D1568494

The Third Emancipation:
A New People — A New Clan

by Hallie L. Gamble

To:
My Friend,
Marsha
5/27/18

Hallie

DORRANCE
PUBLISHING CO
EST. 1920
PITTSBURGH, PENNSYLVANIA 15238

Dorrance Publishing Co
585 Alpha Drive
Suite 103
Pittsburgh, PA 15238

Visit our website at *www.dorrancebookstore.com*

ISBN: 978-1-4809-5101-3
eISBN: 978-1-4809-5078-8

ACKNOWLEDGEMENTS

I would like to thank all of the friends, co-workers, and family members who pre-ordered *The Third Emancipation: A New People — A New Clan* sight unseen; you believed in my writing ability and I trust that you will not be disappointed in the book. Thanks to my sons, Glenn and Eric, my best friends, for your encouragement and to my Middle Passage ancestor, whose spirit inspired me to seek the answer to my youthful question, "Who am I?" To my grandchildren and my daughter-in-law whom I love dearly, thanks for being you. To my five siblings, thanks for "putting up with me" when at times I practiced the art of teaching on you. To my nieces, nephews, and fellow American Africans, thanks for keeping the contributions of our slave ancestors alive. But most importantly, thanks to the One Who keeps me day-by-day, my LORD and Savior, Jesus Christ. Finally, to my parents, Lizzie and Bob, thanks for the farm—the "place."

Hallie L. Gamble

Family Reunions

Family reunions are important cultural events. In Aqueea's community, it was a major celebration. The family reunions in her community were tied into the local church's "homecoming" worship service, an annual event that took place at her home church on the second Sunday in August every year. Since other churches in the area had homecoming worship services too, the churches scheduled their homecomings around each other so that worshipers could travel a circuit, or the union as it was called, and support each other in their worship service.

All during the week leading up to the homecoming service, folks would start arriving from out of state, New York, New Jersey, Maryland, California—from wherever they'd moved to after leaving the community in order to participate in their family's reunion and attend the homecoming worship service. It wasn't unusual for five or six generations of family members to be in attendance, including the offspring of the family member who moved away. It was typically the older people who'd moved away and enjoyed coming back to homecoming service the most because they got the chance to meet and greet people still living in the community with whom they'd grown up.

Picnics, baseball games, fishing, and other such activities were planned by the church community to entertain the home-comers. Individual families planned their own activities, too. Traditionally, when they gathered for their own reunion, they would have some artifact to represent their family, i.e., t-shirts, hats, pens, etc. During their private time together, families would collect a contribution from each family branch for a family donation to the church in the name of their family's matriarch or patriarch. Family donations were acknowledged during the Sunday morning worship service. Often friendly competition occurred between families to see whose family contributed the most money.

The local church members would start planning the next year's homecoming service soon after the current one was over. The congregation's intent was to come up with a project that would be made on the church, in the church, or around the church so home-comers the next year would be able to see how their contribution from the year before had been used.

The community Aqueea had been born into was a strong one. The local church, a red brick structure, had been built during the post-emancipation era. At least one family in the church community was freed before the Emancipation Proclamation was signed. The three-room school, Averett Graded Elementary School, Aqueea attended was across the yard from the church. After schools were integrated, it had been purchased by the local Prince Hall Averett Union Lodge No. 235 of which her dad was the Grand Master. If some families have been able to trace their lineage back to the Mother Land as Alex Haley did and as Dr. Henry

Louis Gates, Jr. did for Oprah in *Finding Oprah's Roots: Finding Your Own*,[1] there are others who haven't. For example, Emmitt Smith, the former American football player, National Football League's all-time leading rusher, three-time Super Bowl champion, *Dancing with the Stars'* winner [2] traced his roots to Boydton, Virginia, the county seat for Mecklenburg County, Virginia. There he found out that meticulous records were kept of the bloodlines of horses, but not for slaves; consequently, his search didn't provide links that could lead his roots back to the Mother Land. As a matter of fact: "Mecklenburg was an early horse-breeding and racing region in America. Racing was important to the lives of the people of Mecklenburg. Race day was a day of socializing, gambling, eating, and heavy drinking. Races would continue for three to four days. The county had numerous quarter mile, mile, and four mile tracks. Both the towns of Christiansville and Boydton had oval race tracks with rails', infield, and grandstands.'"[3]

MECKLENBURG COUNTY, VIRGINIA

Mecklenburg County, Virginia in the mid-1700s was backcountry —the frontier. Small farmers lived there. They grew their own food, raised their own animals, and lived off what they had. If they had slaves then, they had fewer than a dozen. When they made purchases from a merchant it was for items they needed to sustain their farms such as tools, cans, jars, spices, and condiments to season and preserve their food. The few clothing items that

---

[1] Gates, Henry Louis, Jr. Finding Oprah's Roots: Finding Your Own, Crown Publishers, New York, NY 2007

[2] www.oprah.com/oprahshow/emmitt_traces_his_family_history

[3] Watkins Family Information from Andy Watkins – awatkins6@gmail.com

were not made from weaving their own fabrics, they bought to treat themselves to some fashionable apparel. Roads were dirt and often unusable because of being muddy and quicksand-like after rainy or snowy weather. They pretty much were isolated from the rest of the counties in the Virginia colony.

In the 1720s, William Byrd II surveyed the borders between Virginia and North Carolina, the area where Aqueea grew up. While surveying, he came across four springs of water and evidence that a herd of buffalo had recently been there. The water from the springs was Lithia water; Byrd spoke about how pleasant it was to the taste and refreshing to the body. In 1728, "He decreed that this was now Buffalo Springs."[4] Later, he built a hunting lodge in Mecklenburg County, which he named Bluestone Castle, where he and his friends would come for hunting.

The Lithia in the waters from the springs at Buffalo Springs were said to be medicinal, providing relief from health conditions such as stomach, bowel, kidney, bladder, liver, and skin conditions.

As time went on, entrepreneurs built resorts around the springs attracting famous people from around the world to it. At the height of its popularity, it grew from being just an eighteenth century ordinary – a tavern or eating house—to a fully functioning nineteenth to twentieth century resort featuring spas and entertainment from well-known performers. The resort featured, among other buildings, a hospitality house and a dining hall.

The fame of the Lithia water at Buffalo Springs was acclaimed worldwide. To accommodate transportation for the large number of people visiting the resort, the railroad operating

[4] Shadows on the Roanoke-William Byrd-Buffalo Springs, https://www.discoversouthside.com

through that section of Mecklenburg County created a branch line at Buffalo Junction. The Buffalo Junction station, built in 1905, was a busy station.

Buffalo Springs put this area of Mecklenburg County on the map, but the ushering in of The Great Depression brought about the demise of the resort, the fame of Buffalo Springs, and the busyness of the Buffalo Junction branch line to the spa. Both Buffalo Springs and Buffalo Junction receded to not much more than names on the map with postal addresses.

While on Mecklenburg's frontier, Byrd and his upper-crust companions dined on corn pone, the customary food of slaves. Byrd offered the corn pone to a white worker who was with them one day and the man was gravely insulted.[5] The customary food for Byrd's class was English biscuits and that was what the white worker expected to have been offered. According to Byrd's biographer, the whites at the lowest level in social standing were the most concerned about racial codes and social conduct. They were the lowest class among the whites.

Aqueea surmised that the behaviors of large wealthy planters and white laborers could fall into two categories. Byrd and his friends, she reasoned, had Backcountry-England-Bourgeois mentality. They were comfortable in not eating English biscuits because they knew that they could have them at any time. Therefore, eating corn pone was no big deal with them. They had the wealth to practice the ways of the gentry with land ownership as a pre-requisite. They called themselves gentlemen based on the large plantations they owned. This class was the upper ruling class. Their hands were in the government—the governor's

---

[5] Wiencek, Henry, An Imperfect God: George Washington, His Slaves, and the Creation of America, Farrar, Straus and Giroux, New York, 2004

council, House of Burgesses, church affairs, and Anglican Vestries as well. Their gentlewomen were born into wealth and brought into their marriages to wealthy colonial gentlemen goodly amounts of wealth, which included their personal slaves.

The gentlemen planters, more likely than not, had white managers or relatives as George Washington did, to manager their slaves, grow their crops and maintain day-to-day order allowing them to enjoy the pleasures of life such as horse racing and hunting. "Their barbecues, fish feasts, harvest festivals, and other entertainments brought together and presumably impressed a wide spectrum of their neighbors"[6] from the profits of their plantations. Washington, however, paid close attention to his holdings, keeping a diary in which he recorded pertinent information about his property among which was the dispensing of clothes to his slaves once a year. If these clothes were damaged, out-grown or whatever, the slaves did not get replacements.

The sons of the gentry were sent to Europe to be educated and trained for involvement in colonial economic, political, social, civic, and religious life. The gentry lived in mansions, rode in fancy carriages, and had self-sufficient plantations. All divisions of skilled laborers and craftsmen were among the planters' slaves in addition to their domestic and field slaves.

The planters' lives were that of the aristocracy or bourgeois of Europe. Colonial planters were concerned for the most part with their material interests, respectability, and the maintenance of their status quo class. In other words they had a Backcountry-England-Bourgeois mentality.

---

[6] Gentry in Colonial Virginia; http: www.enclopediavirginia.org

The white worker, to whom Byrd offered the corn pone on the other hand, recoiled and was insulted by being offered corn pone because of his backcountry-frontier mentality, which prevented him from eating the corn pone, even though he might have been starving with hunger. This food was characteristic of or associated with slaves and because of his station in life, which was near or at the bottom of the white social class structure, he would not bring himself to eat slave food in the presence of the ruling class. However, he may have been eating it at his home. Aqueea felt his actions, in effect, demonstrated his backcountry-frontier mentality. Washington gives a further description of what could be considered backcountry-frontier mentality in his encounter with New Englanders who came to fight in the Revolutionary War. According to Weincek: "The embattled farmers of New England did not particularly impress this Southern planter – 'they are an exceeding dirty & nasty people'; and he found an 'unaccountable kind of stupidity in the lower class of these people,' a stupidity shared he thought, by many of the Massachusetts officers."[7]

Byrd and his friends must have had a good laugh at the Virginian worker's rejection of the corn pone when they knew he was probably hungry.

Aqueea was reminded of the story an African friend told her and her son about the Hutus and Tutsis, two African tribes that practiced class status among them, even though they were of the same people. The Hutus were an agricultural people who lived in large family groups. The Tutsis were cattle herders. The minority Tutsis ruled the Hutus. Michael, a member of the ruling class, said that he was playing with a child of the Hutus tribe whose family

---

[7] Wiencek, page 196

7

worked for his parents. One day, he said that he went home with his playmate to eat at the playmate's house. When his parents were told what Michael was doing, they raced to the child's house, snatched Michael up, and beat him all the way back to his house while yelling at him that he should never eat Hutus food because it was poison. Michael said what he could not understand was why his parents beat him and forbade him to eat with his playmate because both families were eating the same food.

In 1700, Virginia had thirteen thousand slaves; in 1730, forty thousand; in 1750, 105,000, of whom nearly eighty percent were Virginia born.[8] The topic of slavery was a big issue during the writing of the Articles of Confederation (1777–1781). After declaring independence from Great Britain, some form of national government needed to be established. Representation and voting were hot issues. Agreement was reached, finally, when the representatives decided to have state-by-state voting and proportional state tax burdens based on land value. The Three-Fifth Clause they worked out agreed on counting three of every five slaves as persons but who had no vote. Though counted, these blacks were still property, not human beings in the minds of the slaveholders. The 1860 U.S. Census Slave Schedules for Mecklenburg County recorded a total of 12,420 slaves.[9]

The large number of slaves was directly related to the tobacco industry in Virginia. George Washington's great-grandfather, John, a shipmate, was on a ship that was transporting a cargo of tobacco from Virginia to England when it ran aground during a

---

[8] Ibid.

[9] Freepages.genealogy.rootsweb.ancestry.com/ajac/vamecklenburg, Transcriber, Tom Blake, August 2003.

storm in 1657.[10] The ship needed repairs. It took a long time to get the ship righted and the repair done; a wealthy planter, who was illiterate, was observing John Washington as he worked on the ship. He learned that John Washington could read and write. As a result, Washington ended up marrying the planter's daughter. It didn't take Washington long to find his place among the elite, although he was not a wealthy planter. His ticket into the aristocratic class was literacy.

Tobacco was in much demand in Europe and John Washington knew the trade. Owning land and raising tobacco was the avenue to prosperity and his marriage to Nathaniel Pope's daughter, Ann Pope, opened the door for him. He worked himself into every aspect of Virginia's colonial society and passed down these opportunities to his descendants, which included George Washington.

Raising tobacco is laborious and needs a lot of workers; slaves were the answer for the large acreage of tobacco the planters had. Mecklenburg County was as much slave country as it was tobacco country. Because it was uncultivated backcountry, it had the rich virgin land that was suitable for growing tobacco but tobacco depleted the nutrients in the soil after several plantings. Therefore new ground had to be cleared frequently.

AT MOUNT VERNON

In northern Virginia, George Washington had amassed five farms and through slave labor, he and other Virginians produced more tobacco than did any of the other colonies. Virginia also had more slaves than did any of the other colonies at that time.

---

[10] Wiencek, page 26

George Washington wrote a purchase order for slaves specifying, "...all of them needed to be straight and limber, strong and pleasant to look at, with good teeth and that the males were twenty years old and the females, sixteen years old." Wiencek suggests that: "Washington was growing laborers[11] as if they were a crop, to make himself self-sufficient as a slave owner... Between 1760 and 1774 the number of his taxable slaves more than doubled from 49 to 135."

Slave labor on Washington's estate, five separate farms, was from sunup to sundown. He created job categories among which were:

- House servants
- Black smiths
- Barrel makers
- Gardeners
- Millers
- Distillers
- Seamstresses
- Shoemakers
- Spinners
- Knitters
- Ditch diggers
- Wagon drivers
- Carpenters
- Weavers
- Craft workers

Twenty-eight percent of the slave force consisted of these skilled laborers. Men made up seventy-five percent of this workforce

---

[11] Ibid page 121

group and included the mulattos.[12] Of the field slaves, sixty-five percent were women. He used women to break up new ground, which consisted of digging up tree roots and making the soil smooth enough for plowing. Field hand laborers were expected to hoe, plow, harvest, and build fences. To expedite work, field hands lived on the outlying farms that they worked on.

In Mecklenburg County, Sir Peyton Skipwith, originally from England, built the Prestwould house in 1794. He made his fortune from tobacco too. Among his skilled slaves were wagoners, weavers, and woodmen. Prestwould is said to be the largest plantation in Virginia. A number of the original outbuildings and the garden of his wife, Lady Jean, are now current-day tourist attractions that the town of Clarksville, Virginia advertises. His slave house was a single room structure measuring roughly twelve feet by sixteen feet. Papers and records of the Skipwith family provide insight into slave deeds, lists, and sales agreements of enslaved individuals. Humberston Skipwith, Lady Jean's son had 247 slaves.[13]

William Byrd, II was concerned about how slavery created a mindset in whites that they were above doing work because they felt it was beneath them. He also found that white workers at the lower level were strenuously conscious of any act that might be looked upon as equating them to the level of a slave's standing such as the white worker who was offended when Byrd did not give him English bread but corn pone instead. The wealthy Virginia planters' behavior mimicked the behavior of European aristocrats, which is why Aqueea called the way they thought and acted Backcountry-England-Bourgeois mentality. They had the

---

[12] George Washington's Mount Vernon, http://www.mountvernon.org

[13] Prestwould Plantation, http://www.aahistoricsitesva.org

benefits, generated from the work division of slaves, to have every aspect of living lives of pleasure, as did the aristocrats of Europe. What were missing were the official titles such as the title Sir Peyton Skipwith of Mecklenburg County affixed to his name. Missing also were the accompanying pomp and circumstance surrounding European titles and the societal acknowledgements and acceptance that went with these titles. Since each planter was his own person, sufficient unto himself, the absence of societal sanctioning with whatever he called himself did not bother him. He was a member of the ruling class after all. The colonial period colonists built a society that had aspects of the bourgeois proletarian period. The first influx of English settlers was mostly youths from the lower-middle classes with experience in agriculture and crafts. Land ownership lured them to New England, so named because aspects of the northeast landscape reminded them of England. The colonies offered settlers fifty acres of land, but in Virginia, ten shillings could buy a tract of one hundred acres. Needless to say, land was inexpensive. By1775, the settlers had evolved into a class structure. Ten percent were capitalist: great planters, large merchants, etc., twenty percent large farmers, professionals, tradesmen and other upper-middle elements, forty percent small land-owning farmers, ten percent artisans: blacksmiths, coopers, carpenters, shipwrights, etc., fifteen percent temporary workers, usually soon moving upwards into the ranks of the small farmers, and 5 percent laborers.[14] The first four class structures, at eighty percent, made up the bourgeois and the petit bourgeois class structures.

The great planters had more than one thousand acres of land and built themselves into a class structure that featured every as-

---

[14] https://onkwehonwerising.files.wordpress.com/2013/04/settlers-mythology-of-the-white-proletariat.pdf

pect of an elitist's society. Fathers sent their sons to Europe for their education. They and their offspring and relatives held government positions. "They were all planters, they were all slaveholders, and they spoke for their class, which consisted of themselves and people like them."[15] Not only did they fill government positions but they also were involved in the court systems and churches.

The poor whites on the other hand had backcountry-frontier mentality. They were mostly illiterate, brutish, showed little intelligence, and had crude behavior. Current organizations of post-Civil War southerners still tout titles such as "Knight" and "Lady" and are organized to keep alive the Confederate ideals.[16] *Empire of the Owls* consists of "Reflections on the North's War against Southern Secession."[17] Traywick writes, "...the poor whites never laid aside their hostility towards blacks, bond or free."[18]

The large plantation owners called themselves gentlemen and gentlewomen among whom were George Washington, Thomas Jefferson, and William Fairfax.

EDUCATION

George Washington didn't have the opportunity to study abroad as did his two older half-brothers, Lawrence and Austin. George mostly taught himself. At the age of eleven, he started his own educational pursuits. Three books that he read and practiced living by were *The Rules of Civility*, Seneca's *Morals* and Joseph Addison's tragedy *Cato*. Among the other skills he

---

[15] Wiencek, page 57

[16] Traywick, Jr., H.H., Empire of the Owls; Dementi Milestone Publishing, Inc., Manakin-Sabot, VA, 2013

[17] Ibid cover page

[18] Ibid page 315

taught himself were dancing, fencing, and riding. William Fairfax gave him books to help him polish his manners and further develop his intelligence. However, John Adams is reported to have said that Washington was not literate enough, not well-read enough, and not learned enough to hold the office of president of America.[19]

Washington himself admitted to his consciousness of a defective education. In Virginia, Washington and his peers saw to it that white orphans and bastards were taught reading, writing, and a useful trade, but mulatto children were not taught anything. They were routed to the lowest rung of the laboring class.[20] Laws were passed that prohibited literacy for slaves. When Washington got to New England during the Revolutionary War, he was surprised that not only could blacks read and write, but that they were in uniform as well. The first emancipation of slaves or at least integration could have happened in America then. However, southerner slave owners were repulsed at the thought of blacks whether free or slave, fighting for America.

"Southern slaveholders recognized that the New England army was setting precedents that might later bind them. Hearing that blacks were serving in Massachusetts, Edward Rutledge of South Carolina stood before the Continental Congress in September 1775 to demand that all black men, whether slave or free, be immediately expelled from the armed forces. Other Southerners joined Rutledge in his attempt to thwart integration before it got out of control.

In November of 1775, Washington issued a general order excluding all blacks. Yet on December 30, 1775, he reversed part of

[19] Wiencek, page 59
[20] Ibid, page 129

his order and allowed free blacks to enlist because of appeals made by free blacks."[21]

It would not be until Executive Order 9981 in 1948, signed by President Harry S. Truman, that the military was integrated.

The basis for opposition to blacks serving in the Revolutionary War was two-fold, Aqueea thought to herself. One, the Backcountry-England-Bourgeois mentality of the ruling class was that having slaves fight side-by-side with whites reduced whites to slave-status in their minds and dishonored free men who were fighting for freedom. Two, slaves were considered property, not people.

The next surprise for Washington was a letter from Phillis Wheatley, a slave girl, when he was at his Cambridge, Massachusetts headquarters. He'd never received a communication of any kind from a black before. For the first time in his life, Washington met with free blacks that wanted to fight for the cause and a literate slave, Phillis Wheatley, as well. Phillis, thought to be about seven years old and nearly naked, was purchased for almost nothing. She was covered with pieces of dirty carpet when Susanna Wheatley, the wife of a successful Boston tailor, John Wheatley, saw her. The Wheatley family named her Phillis after the ship they found her on.

Nonetheless, Washington, after meeting Phillis, made no move to persuade his southerner peers, which included Thomas Jefferson, who was one of the most prejudicial towards blacks by now, to abolish slavery and make America one country.

Jefferson's position was that blacks could be free but not in America. He felt that blacks should be colonized in some place other than the colonies because blacks and whites weren't meant

---

[21] Ibid, pages 200, 201, 204

to live side by side. He believed African-Americans were biologically inferior to whites and thought the two races could not co-exist peacefully in freedom. [22]

Ironically, Jefferson had written an emancipation bill for Thomas Howell, a black indentured servant who had ran away from his master and was seeking the help of a lawyer who turned out to be Thomas Jefferson. Jefferson, while serving as a burgess from Albemarle County, Virginia, in 1769, had also seconded a proposal that Richard Bland had put forth which allowed slave masters to emancipate their slaves. However, when Edward Coles wrote to Jefferson in 1814, asking his opinion on freeing some slaves he had inherited, Jefferson had changed from the Jefferson he was in 1769. He responded to Coles that, "…it was the duty of every slaveholding gentleman to shoulder the ancestral burden as best he could, for the good of both races: there was no place for free blacks in a slave-based society."[23]

Furthermore, Jefferson believed that blacks didn't have any intellect in spite of the fact that some of the imported slaves were master craftsmen, and knowledgeable of applied sciences, one of which was Benjamin Banneker. Banneker is known to have had communications with Jefferson. Banneker used the Declaration of Independence to argue with Jefferson about freedom and equality and Jefferson's racist beliefs. Banneker, along with his letter of August 19, 1791 to Jefferson in which he asked Jefferson to act on behalf of African Americans, sent a hand-written copy of his almanac for Jefferson's perusal. Jefferson's August 30, 1791 response to Banneker's letter was as follows:

---

[22] https://www.history.com/topics/us-presidents/thomas-jefferson

[23] https://www.nytimes.com/2005/08/07/books/review/setting-them-fr...

"Sir, I thank you, sincerely, for your letter of the 19th instant, and for the Almanac it contained. No body wishes more than I do, to see such proofs as you exhibit, that nature has given to our black brethren talents equal to those of other colors of men; and that the appearance of the want of them, is owning merely to the degraded condition of their existence, both in Africa and America. I can add with truth, that no body wishes more ardently to see a good system commenced, for raising the condition, both of their body and mind, to what it ought to be, as far as the imbecility of their present existence, and other circumstances, which cannot be neglected, will admit.

I have taken the liberty of sending your Almanac to Monsieur de Condozett, Secretary of the Academy of Sciences at Paris, and Member of the Philanthropic Society, because I considered it as a document, to which your whole color had a right for their justification, against the doubts, which have been entertained of them.

I am with great esteem, Sir, Your most obedient Humble Servant,

Thomas Jefferson"[24]

Jefferson, in all probability, knew of the skill that existed within the slave population. For example, George Washington was

---

[24] Benjamin Banneker, Thomas Jefferson and the Question of Racial......https://www.every-daycitizen.com

among the small number of planters with more than one thousand acres and as a result, needed a large slave population to run his farms. However, not only was Washington a shrewd planter, he was a contractor as well. He would hire out slaves such as builders, who under the supervision of an overseer would build structures for other planters. Between 1769 and 1814, Jefferson and his Backcountry-England-Bourgeois mentality along with the pressure of his peers upheld the status-quo class standards, overriding the humanistic ideals he initially brought with him to the House of Burgess. Certainly peer pressure from his slave-owning class had tarnished his moral judgment from which he never recovered. According to John Chester Miller, "Jefferson helped to inaugurate the historical tendency in America to invest racial prejudice with the gloss of pseudoscientific verification required in the nineteenth century."[25]

There were, however, individuals in the colonies who did emancipate their slaves. One of them was John Dickinson who manumitted his slaves conditionally in 1777 and unconditionally in 1786.[26] The most notable however, was Robert Carter. Carter was among the upper ruling class and was the aristocrat of Virginia. According to John R. Barden, Carter gradually emancipated more than five hundred of his slaves, the largest individual emancipation before 1860.[27] Andrew Levy in his book, *The Forgotten First Emancipator*, tells the story of this Virginian aristocrat.

THE LUMBER MILL MAN
Ollie Downie worked at the lumber mill that was operating in

---

[25] Wiencek, pages 119-120

[26] http://dickinsonproject.rch.uky.edu/bgraphy.php

[27] http://www.encyclopediavirginia.org/Carter_Robert_1728-1804

Buffalo Junction, an unincorporated area in the extreme southern part of Mecklenburg County, Virginia. This part of Mecklenburg County bordered North Carolina in the south and Halifax County, Virginia, on the west. It was very rural and one of the poorest parts of the county but stands of hardwood and softwood trees were plentiful. Interspersed like patchwork quilts were open fields and pastures in Buffalo Junction and neighboring Nelson, another unincorporated community under the administration of the County of Mecklenburg.

One day, the lumber mill man, Mr. Larks, took Ollie with him to survey a farm in Nelson, Mecklenburg County, Virginia; an area located about four miles from the lumber mill he ran at Buffalo Junction. The farm had stands of hardwood trees and several kinds of young trees—oaks, maples, birch, and poplar as well as softwood trees such as pines, firs, and spruces. Nut trees were black walnut, hazelnut, pecan, and hickory. Larks walked the entire farm, visually inspecting and marking trees for cutting.

After marking the trees, they were standing in the yard of the farmhouse when Mr. Larks spoke. "Ollie, I been watching you. I like the way you work."

"Thank you Mister Larks," Ollie responded. "I try to work my best all the time. I have a lot of mouths to feed."

"I heard you just had another one," Larks said with indifference. "How many you got now?"

Studying the man speaking with him, Ollie looked at the red beard covering his face, his steel-toed boots, the red plaid lumberjack jacket he was wearing, and the matching cap that covered most of his red hair, which came down below the nape of his neck. His huge hands were covered with well-worn leather gloves and even though he was covered in protective lumber gear, the muscles of his arms and legs were clearly defined. Ollie had seen how Larks could cut underbrush and fell trees.

Every part of the farm, over a hundred acres, was being clear-cut. Nothing would be left but saplings, rotten trees, undergrowth, and the mature trees that had to be left which were along the banks of Buffalo Creek.

The creek separated the back part of the farm from the front, which was bordered by the rural state road. As he did his walk-through, Larks had found a spot where a logging bridge could be put across the creek so that logs from the back part of the farm could be hauled to a cleared area on the roadside and loaded onto the logging trucks that would transport them to the lumber mill.

Ollie had been taught by experience how to fell a tree since he'd grown up on a farm. Cuts made near the base controlled the direction the tree would fall; after felling, the limbs were trimmed off with a chainsaw and then the tree was cut into transportable log lengths. Ollie was just as knowledgeable of cutting trees as Larks, but he let Larks be the teacher; it was no problem for him to follow Larks' lead.

After the farm had been mostly stripped of its mature hard and soft woods, uncultivated fields and pastures hidden behind stately trees now were exposed. Farm buildings were in need of repair and a farmhouse waiting for a family to occupy it stood lonely and empty. The yard surrounding the front of the farmhouse had hedges that were almost as tall as trees. A weed-covered orchard was across from the side yard and two black walnut trees, one next to the smokehouse and the other near the dining room, were full of young walnuts.

The one thing that Ollie really was impressed by was a well that was just outside the farmhouse. He'd never seen anything like it. Huge cement blocks formed a porch surrounding the well and the porch connected directly to the house. Ollie wondered what a majestic place the farm must have been when it was a working farm. He imagined how happy his wife, Lizza, whom he called Funny or Momma, would be with a well of water right at her door. *Could I ever dream of such a thing?* he thought to himself.

Quickly, his attention turned to Mr. Larks' comments. Ollie thought that maybe Larks was leading to laying him off after cutting every piece of sellable timber on the farm.

"I have six mouths to feed, Sir," Ollie replied.

"Ollie, I'm not married and I don't have any roots around here, do you?"

"Yes, sir, been 'round here all my life and my mommy and papa's from 'round here, too."

"I see," Larks said. "What if I sold this place to you?"

"Sir?" Ollie exclaimed as if he'd been punched in his stomach and his breath had been knocked out of him.

"Well, are you interested?" Larks asked the stunned man.

"Yes, sir, Mister Larks. I would be right pleased but I can't pay you," Ollie responded with remorse as if he'd been asked to have a nice piping hot slice of apple pie, his favorite dessert, if he could pay for it. It was a taste and smell so sweet his mouth and soul salivated but if he had put his hand in his pant pocket for money, the only thing there would have been the lint left behind from being washed.

The next words from Larks' mouth sent his emotions into a whirlwind. His thoughts were a windstorm of possibilities.

"We could work out something," Larks said. How much cash do you have?

Acting as dignified as he could, he answered quietly, "Well, sir, I try to save as much as I can each time I am paid the little bit of money I get. I think that in the last ten years, I managed to save up around five hundred dollars. That's all I have to my name." He felt the wind of his dreams blowing away, scattering as if caught in a whirlwind; then Mr. Larks spoke again.

"Well, that's enough for a down payment," Larks replied, with a soft chuckle.

"But how I'm gonna pay the rest? The bank won't let me have any money."

"Ollie, we'll see about that." Suppose I put a word or two in for you at the bank? I do a lot of business there," Larks answered.

"But now that the clear cuttin' almost done, ain't you planning to lay me off, like you being doing the other colored men helping you?" Ollie asked.

"I told you I like the way you work and how you carry yourself," Larks responded. "If I put you on at the lumber mill, you will be around a lot of white boys. When they start hounding you, what you gonna do?"

"Mr. Larks, I been 'round white folks all my life. Like the rabbit and the coon, I learned to duck and hide and hold my own when I get tree'd."

Mr. Larks laughed heartily at Ollie's trope; the two of them were standing in the part of the yard where six huge blocks of cement surrounded a well and formed a well porch. Ollie looked again at the well porch, which connected directly to the house. He marveled at what he witnessed and thought, *Funny is gonna love this.*

She's gonna be the only one 'round with a well like this. What would Funny do if she had something like that? The dream of his wife owning a well like he'd never seen before was about to become a reality.

"Come on in," Mr. Larks said as he stepped onto the large circular wheel of cement that had a hole in the center of it and served as a step to the well porch. "Let me show you inside the house," Larks said as he pulled open the door that led from the well porch. He and Ollie stepped into a large room that had one window in it, which faced the door off the well porch. A door was at each end of the room. A fireplace was near the door at one end of the room and another porch at the end of the other; the fireplace chimney was shared with the chimney in the next room, the kitchen. The kitchen had one window that looked out to where the smokehouse was and a door that faced the path that led to the stable and some of the other farm buildings. Larks caressed a large wood-burning cookstove that was connected to the chimney in the kitchen and showed Ollie how it worked. It had four eye plates. Firewood could be put in the firebox using the two eye plates over the firebox or by opening the firebox door at the front of the stove. The other two eye plates were for making it easier to clean soot and ashes from the fire chamber and for keeping food warm when placed on them. At the end of the stove opposite the firebox was a large water reservoir that held about five gallons of water. A shelf above the back of the stove reached across the entire back of it. It had an enclosed cabinet with sliding doors where food could be stored. The oven had two racks that could hold rather large baking pans.

Composing himself after his emotional description of the cookstove which was like new, Larks told Ollie that he would take him to the bank the next day and that he should bring the five hundred dollars with him. It dawned on Ollie that Larks had had plans for living on the farm. He wondered what happened.

As an afterthought, Larks turned to Ollie as he stroked the stove once again and said, "By the way, I'm leaving the stove here." Ollie s heart was pounding with excitement. He hoped that Larks could not hear the galloping of his blood rushing through his veins. *Surely*, he thought, *I must be having a dream vision*. His mouth was so dry that he could hardly get out a "That's mighty nice of you, Mister Larks." Ollie was almost at the point of tears; his wife would not only have a well connected to the house, but a grand cookstove too. *Lord, what have I done to get this blessing?* he thought to himself. The two men left the kitchen and headed through the dining room to the door that led to a roof-covered porch. This porch was connected to the original part of the house.

"Let's look at the other part of the house," Larks exclaimed as they walked onto the roof-covered porch. Each side of the porch was open, one side to the driveway, the other side to an inner yard that was between the well porch and steps leading to the central hallway of the original two-room house.

"This porch or the corridor as some folks call it, was added on later," Larks told Ollie. "You can see how you have to step up into the original part of the house here," he said as he reached to open the door to that part of the house. The door was made of two boards that were each about eighteen inches wide. Truly it was a massive tree that the boards were made from. Stepping into the room, Ollie saw that a fireplace was centered at the end of the room that faced the driveway. A small window was on the fireplace wall near the door. Directly across the room when entering from the corridor were two side-by-side windows that overlooked the front yard. Another door, directly opposite the fireplace, led out of the room to the central hallway. The central hallway connected the first room to another room that was the same size as it. This room had a fireplace and three windows, two overlooking the front yard and one overlooking the inner yard. A door was at the end of the central hallway that led to a front porch and the front yard that was surrounded by over-grown hedges. Just before the front door was the entrance to an enclosed staircase, which led to the upstairs rooms, each one above one of the downstairs rooms. There was one window at the front yard end of the upstairs staircase landing and a small hall that separated the two upstairs rooms. One small window was at the end of each room. A small, enclosed closet was under the foot of the staircase and was accessible from the central hallway. The house was built on the order of typical homes of the late 1700s. The structure was about twenty feet by forty feet.

There was an earthen root cellar under the room that was connected to the corridor part but it could only be reached from the inner yard by crawling under the house from an opening in the foundation that was beside a set of steps that led to the central hallway from outside. After getting under the house, there was a ledge that separated the root cellar from the underpinning of the other room. The cellar floor sloped gradually downward until it was deep enough to stand erect at the far end of it. Chicken would go underneath the space opposite the cellar to rest during the heat of the day. When eggs were being gathered, one of the children had to crawl underneath this part to search for any eggs wayward hens may have laid, because they refused to or were too lazy to go to the chicken coop to lay their eggs in the egg boxes.

After Larks and Ollie finished their tour inside the house, he led Ollie back to the well porch.

Looking at Ollie with a stern face, he said, "Ollie, you see that my purpose is to fell every tree that I can get something from. After I finish, I plan to move on. It will be another thirty or forty years before the saplings I leave will be of any value. But if you look at the open fields and the pastures you see that with some hard work, you can make the farm take care of your family."

Pointing to the structures on the farm, he described them all to Ollie. He explained that the smokehouse across the yard from the kitchen had a fire pit in the middle of the floor to cure hickory-smoked meat in the spring, a salt box to pack fresh meat in, and hooks suspended from the ceiling to hang meat for smoking and to keep it safe until it was needed. Next, he pointed out the two-stalls stable that had an overhang so a wagon carrying hay could pull under it to pitch hay into the loft and not have to worry about the elements. Inside the stable were two feeding troughs, one for each stall and an open floor in front of the feeding troughs where more hay could be stored. Next to one trough there was a ladder that led up to the loft. He showed Ollie the open windows on each side of the stable so that animals could be observed without having to open the stable doors. After that, Larks walked Ollie around the other structures—the pigpen, cowshed, corncrib, tobacco pack house, chicken coop, toolshed, and the tobacco barn.

"Come on, I might as well walk you to the fields too," Larks told him. "Why don't we start by the stable?" The two men turned around and walked back in the direction they'd just come from.

They walked past the farmhouse again, the smokehouse corn-crib, pigpen, stable, and the toolshed, which stood across from the stable and the cowshed that was inside the pasture. The weeds grew everywhere. The pathway could barely be seen.

Larks, pointing to his right with his back to the structures, said, "That field is about ten acres there. It's good for planting corn." Then pointing straight ahead he told Ollie that hay could be planted in the front and corn at the back of that same field.

They walked towards the cowshed that was across from the stable. The cowshed structure had two stalls and was inside the pasture next to the pasture gate. Three strands of barbed wire ran from the cowshed following a path that curved alongside the fields Larks had pointed out and disappeared behind a grove of trees. There were more fields that followed the fence, separated by a grass-covered roughed-out road just wide enough to pull a wagon through. Larks said that either corn or tobacco could be grown there.

He reminded Ollie of the three fields beyond these down by Buffalo Creek. Walking the path that was beside the barbed wire fence, they descended a small hill that bordered another field that was about eight acres. Trees grew at the outer edges of all the fields and had been marked for cutting.

"Ollie," Larks said, "We won't walk down there but you can see through the trees more fields. I call them the three cornfields. Each one of those fields is about five acres apiece. So you see, there's plenty opportunity to raise corn and hay for your livestock. There's another good-sized branch that runs into Buffalo Creek down there and since those fields flood you may just wanna plant corn in them. That's about it over on this side of the farm." Turning back towards the house he told Ollie that they would walk the land on the side opposite of where they were.

They walked the path that led back to the stable, the toolshed, the cowshed, the pigpen, and the corncrib, next to a little patch of land used for gardening, that was between the corncrib and the woodshed, past the woodshed and the smokehouse, across from an orchard, down a little knoll, and past a tobacco barn. The barbed wire fence at the cowshed ran behind the farm structures there and followed along this area too.

As Larks and Ollie descended another little knoll after passing the tobacco barn, a field opened up.

Looking at Ollie, Larks said authoritatively, "Aside from timber, I raise cattle, so you see that that same barbed wire fence you saw on the other side where we just came from continues over here. It runs along Buffalo Creek at the back end from down here all the way back over to the three cornfields, then up to the cowshed. You could have a small herd and a couple of milk cows. If you noticed, all the fields are sheltered on every side with trees. Planting tobacco here should be okay. And right there by the fence, if you clear a space, your tobacco plant bed could go there. This field would be good for planting your tobacco crop. It would be good for planting wheat, too. By the time you need it for tobacco, the wheat would be ready for cutting."

All Ollie could say was, "Thank you, sir." Larks had no idea of the possibilities Ollie envisioned for how the farm would be used. For one, Ollie could see how he now could fulfill the dream of sending all six of his children to high school—something he and his wife never had the chance for; they only had an elementary education. He made a silent promise to himself that his wife would never work for white folks and his children wouldn't either. Larks drew him out of his deep thoughts, and he looked in the direction that Larks was pointing.

"Now you remember when you was walking down through here with me, Buffalo Creek gets pretty wide." They walked down another little path that was bush-covered on both sides at the foot of which was another field. Looking Ollie in the face, Larks continued, "That field down there is right on the creek bank. Just a few saplings and undergrowth separate it from the water. They called it, Will Royster flat, named after William Royster. By the way, the town of Clarksville is named for his son, Clarke. Anytime there's a downpour from a thunderstorm, you can expect this area to flood too. This here creek is called Buffalo Creek 'cause when a heavy downpour comes, it's like a herd of stampeding Buffalos. It uproots trees along the bank and sweeps 'em downstream as well as anything else in its path; cucumbers would grow well down there. Another cash crop that could help support ya'll."

"Yes, Sir," Ollie who was practically speechless by now responded, directing his eyes slightly past Larks, not returning his look into Larks' eyes. He thought to himself, *I think I oughta pinch me to see if I'm having a spell.*

Again, pointing to where the rural road and the bridge crossing Buffalo Creek were, Larks said, "On the other side of Buffalo Creek there, the property follows the road 'til it crosses Buffalo Creek again over there by the three cornfields." He turned to show Ollie the direction of the property line as he spoke.

"If you remember, there was no fields over there on the other side of the creek, just trees. But it's a good mix of hardwoods and softwoods over there. If you let the saplings grow, in time you'll have a nice tree crop for harvesting and can get just as good a clear-cutting as me."

Larks, a well-educated, savvy businessman, laced his speech with broken English at leisure.

As they walked back up to the farmhouse yard, Ollie fought back tears of joy. When he thought he had a moment of privacy, he clapped his hands together, which made a loud *pow* and exclaimed, "Thank you Jeeeesus." What Larks didn't know was that Ollie had that five hundred dollars because his plan was to move north. The last thing he wanted for himself and his family was to become sharecroppers and at that time, moving north seemed to have been his only option.

Mr. Larks, knowing that Ollie thought he was out of ear shot from him, quietly chuckled to himself.

"Now, before we get on back to the mill, I just wanted to point out the orchard. You see there's several types of apple trees hidden in all those weeds over there," pointing to a group of trees beyond the porch corridor and across the driveway. "There are some peach trees, a few cherry trees and one or two pear trees in that grove." Walking past the smokehouse down towards the chicken coop, he pointed to a damson tree and two mature pear trees that were loaded with fruit. "Now besides these pear trees, behind the tobacco pack house inside the fence is a nice stand of plum trees. They make good plum jelly and preserves. By the way, up there behind the stable, all along the field edges, some fine blackberries can be picked."

Ollie hadn't noticed the orchard but he had seen the huge black walnut trees, one on the dining room side of the house and the other near the smokehouse. The walnuts were difficult to crack open but once the meat, or the goodie, as he called it, was baked and slightly salted, they made an excellent snack. If a cupful could be saved, Lizza would bake the most delicious black walnut cake he'd ever sunk his teeth into. He had also spotted a couple of pecan trees in the area of the corncrib almost hidden from view by the weeds and undergrowth that had invaded every corner and crevice of the farmhouse yard, garden area, and orchards.

"Beyond the orchard there," Larks said as they stood in the yard, "those trees follow the property line back down to another small branch. Then the line comes back up there in front of the house and goes back over against that hill and comes back around to those trees behind the fields there past the stable."

The marking of a few additional trees to be cut and the tour of the farm completed, the men climbed into Larks' truck and headed back to the lumber mill.

Neither man spoke to the other and if Larks had spoken, in all probability, Ollie would not have heard him. His mind was on what had just happened. No way would a black man have been given the chance to buy a piece of property in this community, let alone a piece of real estate as valuable as this farm.

THE HOUSE AT BUFFALO JUNCTION

The family hadn't moved to the farm when Aqueea woke up to the day that would change her life. She was surprised to see her mom still in bed. Since her siblings weren't there, she supposed that they'd left for school. Even more to her surprise, her dad was still at home. Usually he would be out of the house before the older children left for school. Her dad, a soft-spoken person except for when he was questioned by his children or angry, must have seen the puzzled look on Aqueea's face.

Before she could speak, he said, "Your mamma ain't feeling well this morning. I got everybody off to school. Yo food's on the table. Go eat."

Aqueea, a slender, well-proportioned five and a half year old with chocolate-colored brown skin had big dove-like eyes. She had long black curly hair like her mom's. Her hair was plaited into three braids and needed combing. She had on a well-worn, hand-me-down nightgown.

Crawling out of her cot bed, which was in a corner of her parents' bedroom, she got on her knees, said her morning prayer, and then headed for the kitchen without saying anything. She didn't want to cross her dad. She knew to do what he said and to ask no questions.

The other children, Aqueea's siblings, two boys and two girls, shared the bedroom across from their parents' bedroom. Their birth order was girl, boy, girl, boy and their ages were no more than a year or so apart. Since Aqueea was three years younger than the brother above her, she mostly was left out of whatever her siblings did because she had a habit of telling on them when they did things they weren't suppose to. She didn't mind being slighted by them because her mom was the stand-in between them and her. They did like teasing her though. One of their favorite tricks at Buffalo Junction was to lure her out of the yard away from the house at dusk. When she came to them, they would run as fast as they could back to the house yelling back to her that they'd seen the Boogie Man. Of course, Aqueea, scared silly, would run back to the house as fast as she could, stumbling along the way because she couldn't see well through her tears, calling out for her mom, "Momma, Momma, they's makin' funky at me!"

Her mom and her dad's father, Grandpa Hamily, who at that time, lived down the road from them not far from the general store, were her two favorite people. Her next favorite was her cousin, Fanny, who lived with Aqueea's Grandpa Hamily and his wife, Elisa. Fanny was stocky, clumsy, and a little on the slow side but loved Aqueea. Her name for Aqueea was Queea. Fanny's mother was Aqueea's dad's sister. She had married one of Aqueea's mom's brothers. So Aqueea told Fanny they were double first cousins.

The three-room house was small with two bedrooms and a kitchen. The larger bedroom was her parents' and it served as the living room too. However, company was also entertained in the kitchen.

In the kitchen was a two-eye wood cookstove. The cooktop had eyes that were covered with two plates. The plate coverings were removed with a lid lifter in order for wood to be put in the firebox of the stove. Two things stood in Aqueea's memory from her childhood. One was that each day when it was naptime, her mom would have to lay down with her. As soon as Aqueea fell asleep, her mom would get up and go about her house chores. Upon awaking, Aqueea would discover that her mom wasn't beside her anymore. She would get up, go find where her mom was, then walk to the kitchen door. She would position herself to where she could see her dad before he came home, which would be right after the whistle at the lumber mill blew to signal that work for the day was finished and she would start crying. Her mom would plead with her to stop crying. Her response to her mom was, "Me cry all me wanna," and she would begin to wail even louder. She continued this until one day her dad left work before the whistle blew and came into the house through the front door, rather than the back door as was his habit. Apparently her mom had told Aqueea's dad about her pouting and crying behavior, which wearied her gravely.

The day he came home early, he found Aqueea just as his wife had said he would find her, at the door watching for him as she wailed. After a good whacking on her bottom, she no longer cried nor did she watch for her dad anymore. She, instead, would go to her favorite corner at the foot of her cot bed when she woke up and sulked there until she got the rest of her nap out of her system.

The next thing she remembered was when she and the brother who was three years older than her were in the backyard playing near the cauldron in which their mom was boiling some bed sheets. They didn't notice that their mom's sister, who'd come in the house through the front door, was standing at the back door watching them. The next thing Aqueea and her brother knew was that their dad came around the corner of the house with a switch in his hand, screaming at them, "Rosetta came to the mill to tell me that you young'uns over here playing with fire! What yo trying to do, burn the house down?" It wasn't enough that she'd lied on them but she stood at the back door watching and laughing at the crying children as their dad whipped them.

Aqueea's mom, an attractive woman with caramel-colored skin and black wavy hair that hung down below her shoulders said she was part Native American. Her natural father had died when she was a baby she was told. Her mother re-married, but it was her five natural brothers, she said, who raised her. An outdoors person, she could hunt, fish, can, preserve, find herbs in the forest for healing and practically work magic with her healing hands, plow a straight row with a mule, and plant and harvest crops as well as if not better than any man could.

One of her healing hands feats was manifested after they'd moved to the farm. She found one of her ducks that a hawk had tried to catch; by the time she spotted the wound on the duck's neck, maggots had gotten in it and a big hole was in the duck's neck. Aqueea's mom cleaned up the duck's neck with some of her herbal ointment and kept it penned up until the wound on its neck healed. When the duck was set loose it became the badass boss of the poultry flocks. Aqueea's mom would shell several ears of corn in a pan, mix in some kernels of wheat, and would spread it on the ground broadcast style by letting a small amount slip from the palm of her hand and fingers as she swung her arm forward as if pitching a softball. When the chicken came up to feed, the hole-in-the-neck duck chased them away from the scattered grain until it had gotten its fill. Then the other fowl could eat uninterrupted and her mom allowed the duck to be the boss; after its ordeal, she figured it had earned the opportunity to act out.

The hole-in-the-neck duck may have been the feeding boss, but Aqueea's mom was the ruler of the barnyard and the farm. An incident that showed she was the ruler was when one of her prized roosters had taken up the habit of fighting.

The family raised two breeds of chicken, Rhode Island Reds, a docile, generally easygoing breed and Barred Plymouth Rocks, which grew to be heavier and bigger and were excellent table quality birds. A characteristic of this breed, however, was that they were more aggressive. One cock of the walk was Mr. Cockerel. He was bigger than the usual seven to eight pounds and was dominant, territorial, and overbearing. Aside from the hole-in-the-neck duck, he was a force to be reckoned with. His habit was to run up on his prey and pounce, but if he was seen beforehand, he could be shooed off.

One day coming home from school, Aqueea was walking down the path from the stable towards the house. She was doing one of favorite things—reading a book. Because she was engrossed in the book, which she had stuck up in her face, she was not paying any attention to her surroundings. This territorial rooster that was at least twelve pounds or more, and over a foot and a half inches tall, flew up into her face; her book was knocked out of her hands and losing her balance, she fell to the ground, flat on her back. She tried to keep the rooster from pecking her in her eyes as it jumped up and down on her, flapping its wings, clacking and scratching her with its sharp spurs.

Hearing Aqueea's screams, her mom who was in the kitchen cooking could see what was happening when she looked through the kitchen screen door, which was in alignment with the path. She grabbed the broom from the wood box by the chimney where she kept it, dashed out of the kitchen door and ran to the rescue her child before the rooster injured her. Beating the rooster away, she cursed it with vehemence. Dinner the next day was chicken, smothered in gravy, sliced tomatoes, and hot hoecakes. Aqueea loved spooning gravy over her freshly sliced tomatoes and even more to her enjoyment was chewing on soften chicken bones.

When her mom made bread, while they lived in the three-room house at Buffalo Junction, she was only able to bake one pan of biscuits, called hoecakes, at a time. The hoecakes were the size of three regular biscuits. She would sift self-rising flour into the dough tray, open a small hole in the middle of the flour, put in butter and buttermilk and knead the dough. When it reached the consistency she wanted, she would pinch off a piece about the size of a tennis ball, roll it in the palm of her hand and flatten it out by working it into a circle with her fingers, as pizza dough is shaped for a pizza pie. When the dough was about the size of three flattened biscuits she would place it in the greased bottom of her bread pan. After filling the bread pan with three or four hoecakes, she would flatten the dough with the heel of her hand and put the pan of hoecakes in the one-shelf tiny oven for baking. She had to bake three to four pans of the three-biscuit sized hoe-cakes to be sure the hungry mouths of her family's empty stomachs were filled.

When they moved to the farm, her mom was gifted with a grand wood-burning cookstove. The two-shelf oven was large enough for four pans of hoecakes to be baked at one time, two on each baking rack. The cookstove at Buffalo Junction had only the basics, a stovetop and an oven. Wood could only be put into the stove by removing the two stovetop plates. There was no front end that opened directly to the firebox, as did the cookstove at the farm; nor did it have the size or the amenities of the stove at the farm.

In the kitchen of the three-room Buffalo Junction house, a small, floor-standing cabinet stood near the only window in the kitchen and dishes, condiments, and canned goods were stored there. Next to it was a lard can and a barrel. Her parents would buy a sack of self-rising flour and a sack of corn meal from the general store and store the sacks in the wooden barrel. Pots and pans were hung on the wall along with almanacs, calendars that were suspended from a string that run through the middle of them so that they could be hung from a nail, and old handbags her mom didn't use anymore in which receipts and important papers were kept.

Her dad made the kitchen table, benches, and chairs. They were taken to the farm when they moved. Her dad was very handy with tools and made most of what he needed. In making the kitchen table, he used two very wide boards that had been sanded and shellacked that served as the tabletop. The tabletop rested on a rectangular frame of smaller boards that were the length and width of the tabletop. The table legs, fashioned from small logs hewn down to baseball bat size were bolted to the frame and fastened to the tabletop at each edge.

He made two benches, one for each side of the table, which was the same length as the table. The bench legs were the same width as the bench seat. A crude v-shaped cutout was made at the bottom of the bench legs and gave some semblance of artwork to the legs. A narrow board was nailed at the top of the bench leg bracing the bench seat to it; the board was long enough to reach to the lower end of the opposite leg of the bench seat giving stability to the entire structure. Like the table, the benches were sanded and shellacked. This was where the children and guests would sit.

He made two chairs, one for himself and the other for Aqueea's mom. The legs were made on the same order as the table legs, but smaller. The back legs of the chair were taller than the front legs in order to provide back support when sitting; the front legs were seated position height. The chair seat was comprised of two boards cut to fit the chair frame, laid in a v-formation. Two small boards were nailed to the back legs, one just above the seat and the other just below the top end for back support.

Aqueea's dad would sit at one end of the table and her mom at the other, nearest the little cookstove, so she could refill empty food platters and the breadbasket easily.

When they moved to the farm, the handmade kitchen furniture went with them but Aqueea's mom had to get up from the table and go to the kitchen for refills because the farmhouse had a dining room and a kitchen.

Aqueea and her siblings' stomachs would sometimes be growling for the hot hoecakes that had been split open and covered with butter and plum, pear or peach preserves. They would have thick-cut smoked bacon or ham and gravy, fried apples, and scrambled eggs for breakfast most of the time. Vegetables and whatever other meat their mom had—a rabbit trapped in the rabbit box, fresh catfish, an eel, knotted-head minnows, sun perch, or a snapping turtle caught from Buffalo Creek or the nearby river, duck or geese, meat from the smokehouse—would be served for supper (dinner). Beef hardly ever would be on the menu. Dinner (lunch) was mostly a stew that her mom would put on the stove to slow cook that would be ready for eating when the family came in from the fields. Cows were for milk and butter and young bulls and heifers were for selling at the stock market for emergency cash. At one time there was a herd of fourteen cattle on the farm. The extra pigs and hogs were also used for cash support while poultry and eggs were always for family consumption or giving away.

No one came to sit at the table until her dad had come home from work, had washed up, and had taken his place at the head of the table. After moving to the farm, her mom now sat at the corner of the table nearest him and the door to the kitchen. Baby Sista sat at the foot of the table opposite their dad in her high chair. Two children sat on the bench with their mom and three sat on the other bench across the table from their mom. Everybody had his or her place at the table, every day, all the time. Once everybody was at the table, no one ate until Aqueea's dad said grace… sometimes very, very, very, long ones. The practice of saying grace followed them from the three-room house in Buffalo Junction to the farm and was practiced by Aqueea and her siblings when they had their own families.

Aqueea figured that she was about three and a half years old when the family moved into the three-room house at Buffalo Junction.

The family they moved in behind weren't the cleanest of people. Clearly they didn't bother about cleaning up the house before moving. Maybe they didn't care about whoever would be moving in.

Aqueea's mom scrubbed the dingy wooden floors in all three rooms until they returned to a warm golden brown. She washed down the walls and mopped the ceilings. The smoke and soot-coated windowpanes from oil lamps were cleaned inside and out; the house had no electricity or plumbing. The kitchen cookstove, as tiny as it was, was the worst. It had layers and layers of grease on top and several coats of baked-on spills in the oven. No amount of soil could stand up to Aqueea's mom's elbow grease, Octagon soap, and Red Devil lye though.

There was an occurrence, however, that even her mom's white-gloved hand missed. After she had thoroughly cleaned, she noticed telltale signs of bed bug bites on her children.

She took the beds apart, boiled the sheets, blankets, and pillowcases in the big black cauldron that sat over a fire pit outside in the backyard just beyond the kitchen door.

Using a handmade wooden paddle, she stirred in brown homemade lye soap. After rinsing the bedding several times, she hung everything out to dry on the clothesline, which was set up in the backyard.

This was hard work because her mom had to draw water from the well at the back end of the yard to fill the cauldron and the washtub if the rain barrel sitting under the downspout from the roof was empty. The rain barrel was filled with water from the well as a supplement in dry seasons but for a big wash such as this, the barrel would be drained and Aqueea's mom would have to make that trek to the well.

Her mom used a scrub board to wash the family's clothes, but the cauldron and paddle were used for larger things such as the bedding.

After doing all this, her mom still saw the red whelps from bed bug bites on her children the next morning. She was perplexed. So one night, she decided to stay up and watch. To her amazement, the bugs were coming up through the floorboards, crawling up the wall to the ceiling, and then when they had crawled to where they were above the beds, dropped down on the sleeping children.

The next day, she bought an insecticide that she knew she could spray on the walls, the ceilings, the floors, and every nook and cranny in the house and Aqueea's dad sprayed underneath the house. After that, there were no more signs of bed bug bites on the bodies of her brown babies.

After she finished scrubbing and cleaning the house from top to bottom, inside and out, and underneath cleanliness could be smelled everywhere. It could even be smelled in the front and back grassless yards, which she swept with straw brooms, removing broke bottles, sticks, rocks, and anything else that might hurt one of her children. She was fastidious about her children's health and their safety. Her children, her husband, and her home were her pride and joy—her life.

This November morning when Aqueea awoke to find her dad at home, it wasn't long after that her mom's best friend, Miss Callie got there. When Miss Callie got there, she had her youngest child, Nate, with her. Miss Callie, a pudgy mulatto, affectionately called Red-bone, had six children; her five older children were near the same ages as Aqueea's older siblings and Nate was just a little older than Aqueea.

Miss Callie, who was Aqueea's godmother, was a gifted seamstress. She could look at pictures of clothes in catalogs and make them from scratch. When people bought flour, it was packaged in sacks that had pretty designs on them such as colorful flowers, stripes or squares. When the flour was used up, they would give the empty flour sacks to Miss Callie who would open the seams, wash the sacks real good, and iron them. When she got enough matching flour sacks, she would make clothes for the women in the community. For the one-of-a-kind sacks, she would make children clothes—dresses, pinafores, shorts, skirts, jumpers, and blouses for girls and shirts and pants for boys. Miss Callie did all of the sewing for Aqueea's siblings and hers. When any of the women in the community needed a special dress or something for one of their children, they came to Miss Callie but Aqueea had the best of her artistry outside of her own children. After all, she was Aqueea's godmother.

When Miss Callie got to the house, Aqueea was in the kitchen eating her breakfast—a bowl of corn bread broken into small pieces covered with buttermilk, one of her favorite meals. She heard her dad and Miss Callie talking but didn't comprehend their conversation. As soon as her dad left, Miss Callie and Nate came into the kitchen.

Just as her dad stepped outside, Mr. Otto, the black community's self-taught veterinarian and his wife, Miss Esther, a midwife, riding in a wagon being drawn by a two-mule team, pulled up into the yard. Aqueea's dad spoke with them briefly and continued on his way to work.

In the kitchen, Miss Callie washed Aqueea up, rubbed her face, arms, legs, and feet with some oil and combed her hair, tying ribbons at the end of her three braids. She'd made a new dress for Aqueea, which she'd brought with her and slipped it on her. Aqueea put on her favorite white patent leather Easter sandals. The leather had gotten soft and cracked and had lost its gloss but she liked them nonetheless. All of her toes, not just her big toe, hung over the edge of the sandals; yet Aqueea wouldn't part with them.

A broad grin spread across her face as she patted her new dress, whirring around and around the kitchen floor chanting, "I'm pretty, I love my dress. Thank you Miss Callie."

Aqueea thought that she was the most special person in the world. Her mom, Miss Callie, Fanny, and her grandpa were her nearest circle of love. Whenever she went to her grandparents' house, she would look for her Grandpa Hamily because her favorite thing was when he would pat her on her head and ask, "How's my bright-eyed brown Sugar today?"

With Fanny, who was deathly afraid of water, Aqueea loved luring her to the spring of water that was between the road and their grandparents' house. Pretending to see something interesting, she would beg Fanny to come see it.

"I ain't," Fanny would yell at Aqueea. "You just fooling me Queea."

"No, I ain't," Aqueea would retort. "Come on. Wow! Look at that," as she pointed toward the water was her most compelling response to peak Fanny's curiosity. Having enticed Fanny nearer to the water, she would scoop up a handful and splash Fanny in her face causing her to freak out. Aqueea, knowing that Fanny would be coming after her, ran as fast as she could to find her grandpa who would shield her from Fanny. Fanny never was able to catch up to her though because while she was wiping the water from her face with her dress, Aqueea would have gotten a good head start running from her.

When Miss Callie had finished dressing Aqueea, she took a note out of her pocket and gave it to Nate.

"Nate," she said to her son, "Take this note to the General Store and give it to Mister Gene. Tell him hurry cause these things, we need 'em right away." The "we" Miss Callie referred to was herself, Aqueea's mom, and Mr. Otto's wife, Miss Esther.

Miss Callie led the two children out the back door and walked them around to the front yard. She placed five pennies in Aqueea's hand and told her she could buy herself some candy with it. Aqueea knew exactly what she was going to do with her coins. She'd seen grown-ups do it and today, she planned on doing it too. It was her turn to act like the adults did.

Miss Callie watched the two youngsters as they walked from the yard to the dirt road that ran past the lumber mill house to the General Store. She observed them as they headed down the road; seeing that they were well on their way, she turned around and walked back to the house entering the front door.

It was a long walk to the General Store. The children would have to pass Aqueea's grandparents' house on the way. She wondered if she would see Fanny. If she did, she planned on showing her coins to Fanny and teasing her for not having any. Fanny was the only person she could pick at. Aqueea did to Fanny what her older siblings did to her but she wasn't mean to Fanny like her siblings sometimes were to her.

Aqueea's imagined fun with Fanny left her imagination as quickly as it was imagined. Her thoughts went to her grandma. Her Grandma Elisa always wore a head wrap on her head and an apron around her waist and she talked a lot about people who could conjure. Aqueea didn't know if she had ever put a spell on her but she knew she was not very fond of her because she was famous for giving Aqueea a cleaning out—castor oil mixed with freshly squeezed orange juice, or black draught syrup. All Aqueea knew was that those concoctions griped her stomach terribly. She was always weak and sickly following this ritual, done at least twice a year in spring and winter. Even after they'd moved to the farm, Grandma Elisa would have Aqueea come to her for a cleaning out. Aqueea reasoned that this must have been a conjuration that Grandma Elisa did on her.

Her mind didn't dwell on either her grandma or Fanny for long, but returned to what her goal at the General Store was going to be.

Loam colored dust rose from the dry road bed as Nate and Aqueea ran some, skipped some, and slowed down to a hurried walk some as they hastened to the store. The dust sticking to Aqueea's oiled feet and legs made it look as if she were wearing ginger-colored tights. They looked as though a washcloth had never touched them and she was careful not to abrade her toes on loose stones.

This November day was like summertime; as a matter of fact, folks called this season Indian summer. It was as hot as summer during the day but at night the temperature would drop. Sometimes there would be frost on the grass the next morning. Aqueea's mom would begin cooking turnip and mustard greens from the garden after a frost. She said that the leaves of the greens became tender after a frostbite.

After Nate and Aqueea passed by her grandparents' house, they didn't have much further to go to get to the General Store. Again Aqueea dreamed about what she was going to do with one of her coins, fantasizing each segment through her mind what she would say, how she would act and visualizing her every moment. When the General Store was finally in sight, both children broke into a race to see who would get there first. Nate purposefully slowed down because he knew Aqueea would get an attitude if she didn't get there first.

THE GENERAL STORE

The General Store was the only country store in the area. It was located near the train depot. This was farm country. Rolling hills and cultivated stands of trees covered the landscape where crops were not planted and pastures for grazing livestock weren't fenced in. Because many farms could have hundreds of acres, neighbors were often miles apart. Local farmers would take their produce to the General Store and bartered for staples they needed in addition to having an open credit line that was paid in the fall when they sold their tobacco, the area's cash crop. The line of credit was a never-ending debt because as soon as the current year's debt was paid, the next year's line of credit would begin. For blacks or poor white sharecroppers who lived and worked on better-off white farmers' land, the line of credit was a debt that never got paid.

The store was across from the train depot, which was a local attraction. When the train stopped at the lumber mill or passed by it, the conductor, standing in the red caboose, would throw candy or coins to the children that stood along the train tracks. The train came through generally carrying tobacco since this area was along what was called the tobacco road.

Finally arriving at the General Store, Nate and Aqueea mounted the steps that were like most country general stores—a long porch reaching from one end of the front of the store to the other and steps centered at the middle of the porch. Benches, rocking chairs, flower pots with a variety of flowers, spittoons, and an assortment of farming tools decorated the porch. Local white farmers congregated here to gossip about local happenings, their farms, and the next year's crops. Today, some of the poorer whites had taken up residency on the porch; they avoided being around when the more affluent farmers were there because the better-off farmers didn't want the poorer whites in their conversations.

Both Nate and Aqueea knew to say good morning to white folks knowing they weren't going to respond. If the children didn't speak, however, then the whites would have upbraided them and demanded, "Who yur nigger mammy is? We's need to teller u bastord ain't got no mannars." They never asked about black fathers and as far as they were concerned, every black man was a boy or a buck and never was married with a family but rather a stud that went around making babies and not supporting them. These whites were to be avoided as much as possible.

Mounting the steps to the store, Aqueea and Nate greeted the white men sitting around and rushed inside. The store was like most general country stores. Barrels of seeds, grain, nails, bolts and screws, cured meats and fish such as salt cured herring, and other merchandise stood neatly around the perimeter of the large open floor space. On the walls hung women's and children's clothing and denim work overalls for men and on the floor beneath them were counters with glass tops and sliding doors. Counter shelves held dainty scarves, delicate lace gloves, necklaces, earrings, perfume, cosmetics, and other feminine items. The shelves of one section had personal things that pertained to men such as shaving creams and razor blades. In a section by itself were children's merchandise books, toys, crayons, coloring books, puzzles, shoes, and clothing. Hanging from the ceiling were different types of hats—women's Sunday go-meeting hats, farmers' straw hats, hunting caps, and any type of hat people in the area wore.

Things that were not in the store could be ordered from any of the many catalogs sprawled out on a table in a corner. Next to the table was an icebox where bologna and hot dogs, two of his biggest sellers, were kept. Framers who hired day workers during planting and harvest seasons were known to buy loaves of white bread, loose hot dogs or enough bologna to make one sandwich for each worker—the only meal they would have for a sunup to sundown day of work.

A scoop of ice cream could be purchased from five-gallon containers of vanilla, strawberry or chocolate flavors, but the ice cream Aqueea liked more was made by her mom's mom, Grandma Melissa, who lived on the opposite side of the railroad tracks from her son-in-law's parents. She would make homemade ice cream for her grandchildren using a hand-cranked ice cream maker. Aqueea never even considered looking at the ice cream at the General Store because the ice cream her Grandma Melissa made was the best in the world. Aqueea would watch as her Grandma Melissa would pour the vanilla flavored custard that she'd cooked into the ice cream canister after it had been positioned into the bucket that held the ice and rock salt. She alternated layers of ice and rock salt in the bucket once the dasher had been placed into the canister. The hand crank was secured to the canister and locked into the bucket ears. After about half an hour or so of hand cranking, the ice cream bucket would be covered tightly with canvas until the ice cream was ready to be served. Nothing tasted better than Grandma Melissa's homemade ice cream, not even Mr. Gene's variety of flavors.

Even though the General Store was in a farm area, the store carried fruits, vegetables, and canned goods brought in by local farmers. The train crew, its passengers, and visitors passing through, often stopped in to make purchases of these farm-produced items.

Mr. Gene, owner of the General Store, was in his late fifties. He was a somewhat kind, grey-haired white man who wore eye-glasses. A service he provided to the farmers was bartering with them for produce and staples—eggs, milk, cured pork, fruits and vegetables, and canned and preserved jellies and jams—they needed. If the farm items they had weren't sufficient to cover the cost for their needs, Mr. Gene would put the difference on credit with an agreement that the balance would be paid when they sold their tobacco crop. Otherwise, they would have an open line of credit as her dad did because he had a regular job.

A counter was in front near the entrance of the store. The cash register and accounting books were kept here. This was where customers would pay for their purchases and where Aqueea had seen them put money on the counter and ask for change.

Once in the store, Aqueea wasted no time. She went right up to Mr. Gene who was standing behind the counter doing some paper work. Plopping a coin on the counter she excitedly asked, "Can I have change?"

Mr. Gene looked at the coin, then at her. Restraining himself from laughter, he casually opened the cash register drawer, sorted through the coins in a tray, and took out a shiny coin. He placed the shiny penny on the counter, took Aqueea's tarnished change penny, put it into the tray, and closed the cash register drawer.

"How ya'll doing this morning?" he asked the children, who had not greeted him yet.

In unison, both children piped, "Fine."

Nate took the note his mother had given him and handed it to Mr. Gene. After reading the note, Mr. Gene took a brown paper bag off the shelf underneath the counter. As he filled the bag with merchandise from the list, the children looked at the candy assortments trying to decide how they would spend their coins. Aqueea decided to spend all but her new change. She surveyed the selection of sweets and gum. Finally she chose a tootsie pop and three Mary Jane candies. These choices, she concluded, gave her the most for her money; the tootsie pop, once the candy had been sucked off, had a piece of bubble gum at the center and the Mary Jane pack had four individually wrapped candies in it.

"Okay, yo kids," Mr. Gene called out to them sternly after he'd recorded each item in his account journal, "yo better git these things home, yo folks 'll be needing 'em."

The children scurried over to Mr. Gene, placing their goodies and their coins along with them on the counter. He tallied up each child's money and sweets and placed their purchases in a small paper bag and handed them their individual purchases. Nate grabbed the big brown bag by the handles that Mr. Gene had put on the floor in front of the counter and the children left the store as quickly as they'd entered.

Miss Callie had come back outside and was watching for the children. She met them at the edge of the yard. Taking the bag from Nate, she said, "Come on inside."

When they came into the house, Miss Esther was standing by her mom's bed.

"Come here Aqueea, I want you to meet somebody." Aqueea wondered what she was talking about since she didn't see anybody in the room but her mom who was still in bed, Miss Callie, Miss Esther, and Nate. In those days, grownups didn't talk about midwives and babies to children.

Beckoning for her to come closer, Aqueea took a step or two and stopped beside Miss Esther, who then took her hand and guided her to the bed. After Miss Esther got Aqueea to the bedside, she pulled the covers back.

Smiling at her, she said, "Aqueea, meet your little sister," as she pulled the blanket back to reveal the tiny face of a baby in her mother's arms.

"Ain't she pretty?" her mom said weakly. "This is your baby sister."

Aqueea, recoiling from alongside the bed whined, "Where she come from?"

"Miss Esther brought her," Miss Callie quickly chirped.

"Is Miss Esther gonna take her with her when she leaves?" Aqueea inquired.

"No," Miss Esther said to her. "This is yo' baby sista. I brought her but she stays here." None of it made sense to Aqueea. She thought, *How could somebody bring a baby to somebody's house and leave it behind?*

"But I'm the baby," she whimpered.

"Not anymore," Miss Callie chuckled, "Now yo' the knee baby." Aqueea didn't understand the word knee baby, a southern term that meant next to the youngest child.

The last smidgen of the hard candy that was left stuck to the bubble gum part of her tootsie pop didn't taste good anymore. She dropped her Mary Jane candy and her new penny change on the floor. All of a sudden, her enjoyment of going to the General Store, of teasing her cousin Fanny, and of Grandpa Hamily's affection—all the things in her world—had changed.

If Miss Esther brought this ruddy-skinned, doll-sized baby, then who brought me? Aqueea asked herself. She walked to the corner of the room where her cot bed was. Whenever she was discombobulated, a term her mom used to indicate that she was out of sorts since the encounter with her dad, she would retreat to this spot, her safety zone.

Sinking down to the floor, she shifted through her collection of picture books, old catalogs and magazines that Miss Douglas, a friend of the family and local elementary school teacher, had given to her.

When she found one she liked, she started looking at the pictures of people and different faraway places. The familiar scenes she'd pondered over many times before began to comfort her. There was a sense of wonder about what she saw as she picked out the words she knew.

Books now became her best friends. Nonetheless, a haunting question nagged her. *Did somebody bring me to Mama and Daddy? Were did I come from? If Miss Esther brought me, where did she git me from? Who am I?*

Though she was comforted being in her little library, she couldn't shake the question that was in her heart. *Who am I?* As she grew older, the question nagged her even more. It was like walking on her shadow in the mid-day sun.

Aqueea's mom and the kids, now six of them after the birth of Baby Sista, worked the farm while her dad continued to do public work driving a bus, an eighteen wheeler, or working nights in a textile plant. He worked any job that he could get, one after another, to earn additional income—any paying job except working for a white farmer. The farm, in his mind, under his jurisdiction, functioned as a cocoon for his children to protect them and to allow them to develop into wholesome productive citizens.

It was hard but her parents managed to pay off the farm, saw that all six of their children completed high school and even took the family north to visit city relatives on one occasion. Aqueea remembered visiting some of her mom's people who lived in New Jersey.

It was a long trip from the Virginia farm to New Jersey. Aqueea's mom had packed fried chicken, ham, deviled eggs, and homemade rolls. Jugs were filled with water sufficient for the long trip. Some fruit had been picked from the orchard to take along too. Also packed were a coconut cake, a chocolate cake with pineapple filling, and shirt-tail pies. Shirt-tail pies were made by rolling out dough into a thin circle, filling half of the pastry with a fruit filling, folding the other half over the fruit filled half, and using a fork to crimp the edges together. After that, the shirt-tail pies were fried in hot grease until they were golden brown on both sides.

Enough food was packed to last the family until they got back to the farm. There were neither restaurants where they could sit down to eat at a table nor toilets where they could relieve themselves; their dad had to find discreet places off the highway where both needs could be met.

Aqueea's, Uncle Wayne, one of her dad's older brothers who lived in Philadelphia, the one who was helping Ollie for the move north before the farm was purchased, came to visit the farm every summer taking back north as many cured pork hams and pork shoulders he could to sell. He had told her dad the route to take whenever he decided to come to visit them or to move to the city. He also told Ollie that because his family was so large, he should be prepared to feed them himself and sleep with them in his car.

Uncle Wayne, when he came to see her dad, brought with him a list of the names of people who wanted to buy the cured meat. Her dad had built a reputation for his cured meat. His day for hog killing was on Thanksgiving Day. The black farmers in the community worked cooperatively, each helping the other to slaughter their hogs. Mr. Otto, the self-taught veterinarian, a skilled butcher as well, led the group with cleaning and butchering while her dad, an expert sharpshooter, did the killing. Her mom oversaw the meat preparation for salt-packing which consisted of washing the meat thoroughly and rubbing salt into every crevice, before placing it in a large wooden container in the smokehouse, with layers of salt between each piece of meat. Any liquids in the meat would be drawn out as it lay in the container until springtime. When the meat was taken out it was washed and rubbed in seasonings, her mom's recipe which she guarded closely. After that, it was hung on metal hooks that were suspended from the ceiling of the smokehouse, above a pit, which would be filled with hickory wood for smoking the meat. The soundness and flavor of the cured meat could not be matched. The neighbors, on their nearby farms, could smell the mouth-watering odor of frying bacon or smoked sausage as it was being cooked, when the scent flowed out of the kitchen window and the wind picked up the aroma and blew it across the countryside. The meat was truly coveted.

The crew of men and women would come to the farm early on hog-killing day. The men would do the initial cleaning of the animals. Her mom guided the women in sausage preparation and all the other tasks involved in preserving the fresh meat that would be packed in salt for the winter. In the spring, the meat was taken out of the salt box, washed, seasoned and was hung on hangers suspended from the ceiling to be hickory smoked. In addition to other produce grown on the farm, the pork was an important cash resource, all of which was sold except for that which the family needed.

Every aspect of hog killing went as smooth as clockwork. By late afternoon, all the apparatus for the occasion had been cleaned up and put away, the area washed and waste carted far down in the pasture for burning.

Her mom would serve the crew dinner afterwards. It would consist of the freshly prepared meat—tenderloin pork chops, sausage, chitterlings, turnip greens and turnips from the garden, canned fruit, preserves, homemade biscuits, crackling cornbread (cornbread with fried pork skins in it), butter, and cornmeal pudding, one of her delectable desserts made from cornmeal. Kool-Aid, buttermilk or coffee were the only beverages served unless the men had a swig of moonshine whiskey left over, which they used to warm their inners while they were doing their outside work.

When Aqueea's family visited her mom's relative in south Jersey, it was a shock for her. They didn't live in the luxurious dwelling with carpeted floors, fancy furniture, and plush soft beds as she had imagined they would from pictures she'd seen in different magazines and books. They were farm workers. The house they lived in was made of cinder blocks and all but one room had dirt floors.

They also visited other extended family members of both her mom and dad, who lived in Philadelphia, including Uncle Wayne. The city was not too far from the rural south Jersey area where her mom's folks lived. The relatives in the city lived in tiny apartments that had barely enough room for them. Aqueea didn't re-member where she, her five siblings, and her parents slept—whether at relatives' homes or in her dad's car. She did remember that rather than offering food to them, different people would slip into the kitchen, eat, come back out into the living room where they were and another person would slip off into the kitchen and do the same. Food was never offered to the eight members of Aqueea's family. Seeing the cramped living accom-modations her cousins lived in and the absence of play areas out-side, Aqueea understood now why they would act somewhat uncivilized. Chasing the chicken, throwing rocks at the animals and acting like open space made them crazy mad, they had no re-spect for farm living when they came to visit. When Ollie got back to the farm from their trip, he walked to where he and Larks had stood when Larks asked him if he wanted to buy the farm.

Trembling, he clapped his hands together and proclaimed, "Thank you Jeeeee-sus!" The family thought he was happy to be back home like they were. They didn't know how close he'd come to using his last cent to move north.

Aqueea's mom made a point of feeding relatives who came to visit and providing a clean, comfortable bed for them to sleep in if they stayed over night. Furthermore, anybody who visited the farm always left with something—a jar of canned goods, a cured piece of pork, butter, eggs, vegetables, or fruit. No one left the farm empty handed.

When her parents could afford it, they packed the six children in her dad's vintage automobile, which he kept in extremely good condition and would travel some place—the county fair, a movie, a local baseball game or a church outing. He understood engines and did his own maintenance work on whatever vehicle or machinery he owned.

On one of their outings to the county fair, Aqueea participated in a 4-H contest for youths. Her parents had gotten an empty ten-gallon glass jar that pickled pig feet had been in from Mr. Gene. With her mom's help, Aqueea filled it with pear preserves. The preserves were entered in the homemade-jelly or jam and preserves contest at the county fair. Her entry won a blue ribbon.

Aqueea cherished the jar of preserves. When she got married and had her own place, she took the jar of pear preserves, which had never been open, with her. She enjoyed showing and telling her children and friends about the county fair and her blue ribbon winning jar of pear preserves.

Once when her dad took the family to a small traveling circus, she saw her first live elephant. Her dad was holding her by her hand when she saw the baby elephant. He stumbled over a small pine tree and almost fell because Aqueea was trying to get away from the elephant. She didn't see that the animal had a shackle around its leg; nor did she understand that the animal had been trained to go no farther than the chain attached to the shackle around its leg would reach.

Segregation was the law. Racism prevailed in all walks of life in Mecklenburg County as it did throughout the south. Her dad was upset with her about the elephant incident because she made a spectacle of herself and him when she thought the elephant was going to hurt her. The white folks in the area who saw it laughed and called them stupid niggers.

Ollie Downie strove to protect his family from the ugliness of racism as much as he could. He couldn't do anything about segregation but he could control where his children went and what they were exposed to as much as he was able to. He wanted his children to grow up with healthy self-esteems, and not be beaten down by hurtful racist people. The family's first and only long, long trip out of the state of Virginia was that one up north to visit relatives from both sides of the family.

As the farm grew and crops brought good profit, her dad invested in a tractor. He had to sign a note against the farm with the bank in order to get it. Needless to say, his passion was to pay off that note. His farm—the place—was in jeopardy. He was fastidious about paying his bills, which was why he public-worked, to earn a regular paycheck, however small it was. Many farmers had to wait until they sold their tobacco in the fall to pay their debts. Her dad knew that interest charged on those lines of credit left most farmers very little to live off and if they were black, nothing. Many poor whites and even more blacks did not understand lines of credit, interest, real estate taxes, and receipts.

A year or so later, after he'd paid for the tractor, the bank sent her dad a letter telling of its intent to seize the farm because the lien against it for the tractor hadn't been satisfied. Her dad knew that he had paid for the tractor but he knew that he needed the receipt to verify it.

Aqueea's mom was the record keeper. They didn't have a business desk where all business papers could be kept. They didn't even have a designated location where her dad could sit down and write checks. Things were discussed and taken care of at the dinner table.

Aqueea's mom would put papers in a drawer or in a bag or a handbag as she had done while living in the three-room house at

Buffalo Junction. Now that she had a china closet, she'd started putting them on top of it, a new used piece of furniture for the dining room, and sometimes in a drawer of the buffet that was in the dining room, another piece of used furniture. The search began. All the places where that receipt might have been were gone over and over again. No receipt.

Her dad, forlorn and broken, began to lament about all the hard work that had gone into getting the farm—the place, paying for it, then to lose it over a tractor. He knew that he had paid for the tractor and he knew that the people at the bank knew that he had paid for it too. While he sat at the dining room table, his face in his hands to hide his tears, her mom kept looking. She was like that.

"Funny," the pet name he called his wife, "we gonna lose the farm."

In the face of seemingly defeat, Aqueea's mom would fight harder; this challenge was no different. She truly was her husband's strength and the family's leader.

"Ollie, we ain't gonna lose nothing. That receipt is around here somewhere and if I have to tear this house apart one piece at a time, I'm gonna find it." She kept going through pieces of paper, one at a time.

Well, there was this one old handbag, hanging from a nail on the dining room wall that she'd brought with them from the three-room house at Buffalo Junction when the family moved to the farm. It was mostly hidden behind the back of the china closet.

The old handbag could have been easily overlooked. Spotting it, Aqueea's mom took it down and started rummaging through the pieces of papers in it. It was well past midnight, but, wow, she found that receipt in the old half-hidden handbag.

The next morning, Aqueea's dad was standing at the door of the bank waiting for it to open and was the first customer to step inside once it opened. Without hesitation, he walked over to the bank manager's desk and stood by it, waiting for the manager to come out.

Bank employees saw him standing there. A teller came over to him and asked if she could help him with something.

Aqueea's dad said, "No, I'm here to see the manager." The employee tried to get from him the nature of his business, but he replied, "My business is with the manager," and he wouldn't give her any more information.

The teller went to a back office and told the manager, "There's a nigger out there that wants to talk to you. He won't tell me what his business is. What you want me to do, call the sheriff?"

"What's his name?" the manager wanted to know.

"I'll go ask," the teller responded. When the teller returned, she told the manager, "He say his name is Ollie Downie."

"Not Ole Ollie Downie," the manager chuckled. "Watch this nigger beg and plead with me but I'm git me get a nice historical farm from that boy this morning," he said to the teller as he walked out of the back office, "and I hear that he has made that farm a place of beauty."

Walking to his desk, he sat down and shuffled some papers, not greeting Aqueea's dad or inviting him to sit in one of the empty chairs that were in front of his desk. He didn't even look him in the face or acknowledge his presence. It was as if Ollie was just a shadow taking up no space.

"Why you here, Ollie?" he asked. "I suppose you got the letter we sent you 'bout that tractor?"

"Yes, sir," her dad responded, the veins on his temple starting to bulge. Whenever he was really angry, the veins on his temple protruded like fat earthworms. He struggled to remain cool, calm, and collected, although he was trembling to stay in control of himself. He knew that if he gave any sign of aggression, even in his voice, the sheriff, who in all probability had already been alerted and waiting nearby, would come bursting through the door at a moment's notice to arrest him for threating white people.

The bank's manager saw the tremble of her dad's hands and heard the quiver in his voice, which he took as her dad being nervous and afraid. He casually opened one of the desk's drawers, reached in, pulled out a file folder, and laid it on the desktop, still not looking at Aqueea's dad or inviting him to sit in one of the chairs. Blacks and whites couldn't use the same facilities.

Opening the file folder with exaggerated flair, he fingered through the papers in it. Aqueea's dad noticed that there were papers with the names of black people he knew, including his, in the folder.

"Ollie Downie," the manager grinned as he took out the paper that had her dad's name at the top, in bold letters, "That's you, right?" He knew full well what Aqueea's dad's name was. Ole Ollie Downie, as some people respectfully called him, including whites, had gotten himself a reputation for being honest and accountable among black people as well as with white people in the community.

"Yes, sir," he answered softly.

Reflecting on the names he'd seen in the folder, he realized that they were black families that either had a mortgage on their farms or a note on a piece of farm equipment they'd bought around the same time he'd bought his tractor. He knew this because one of the favorite pastimes of the black men in the community was to trade small talk about what they had just bought or were getting done on their farms when they were at the barbershop on Saturdays or after church on Sundays which were the times that the black community congregated.

"You know the place you got belong to white folks, don't you?" the manager said. "As a matter of fact, that land has history."

"Belonged," her dad answered. And indeed the farm did have history. Will Royster's flat, the place Mr. Larks had told Ollie was good for growing cucumbers was the name of one of the founders and Clarksville, the town, was named after Royster's son, Clarke.

The manager, his ears beginning to redden, said roughly, "You had four years to pay for that tractor. That letter we sent you, this here one," he barked as he held up a copy of the letter sent to her dad, "told you that you defaulted on that note. Since you put up that farm as collateral, the bank is taking it. You see, we white folks try to give you people a chance. What do you do? You jolly hop and flop around and think you can just walk away from paying your bills. Now, I have no alternative but to tell you to git off the place. You have thirty days to find yourself a white sharecrop farmer who will take you on. You have some pretty good size young'uns so somebody will grab y'all up pretty quick. And, oh, by the way, if anything on that farm is damaged, you pay for it."

"Sir," Aqueea's dad responded, "I paid for that tractor in two years' time. Here's my paid receipt to prove it, stamped and signed by you. If you don't mind, sir, would you be kind enough to stamp and sign your paper so your paper will be like mine?" At this, the manager's face and his neck joined his red ears.

That night at the dinner table, after an extraordinary long, long, long dinner grace, Aqueea's dad, an excellent storyteller, re-told the incident embellishing on salient points to make the story more interesting.

MECKLENBURG COUNTY, VIRGINIA—BACKCOUNTRY

Mecklenburg County, Virginia, in the mid-1700s was remote backcountry. In 1765, about 410 landowners lived there. The 1860 U.S. Census Slave Schedules for Mecklenburg County recorded a total of 12,420 slaves, 898 free colored and 6,778 whites (NARA Microfilm Series M653, Roll 1394).[28]

The 1860 Census was the last U.S. Census showing slaves and slave owners. When they were enumerated in 1860, the names of slaves were not given. Only their gender, age, and whether or not they had handicaps such as deafness or blindness were reported.

Slaves who were one hundred or more years old were sup-posed to be named on the 1860 Slave Schedule. Of 3,950,546 total slaves, 1,570 were enumerated. The 1870 Census showed the first and last names of freed slaves if they were enumerated. By 1960, one hundred years later, there were 16,717 whites and 14,703 blacks in the county.

The foregoing list shows the names of slave owners in Meck-lenburg County who had more than a hundred slaves:

---

[28] Freepages.genealogy.rootsweb.ancestry.com/ajac/vamecklenburg, Transcriber, Tom Blake, August 2003

- Alexander, Mark Sr.   163
- Baskerville, William, Jr.   119
- Baskerville, William R.   136
- Field, John S., Sr.   112
- Hendrick, Mary A.   115
- Jiggets, David E.   121
- Moss, R.H.   165
- Overbey, R.M.   116
- Skipwith, H.   247
- Terry, Edward   113
- Terry, George   114
- Townes, William   187

Of the 185 slave owners in Mecklenburg County listed in the 1860 Slave Schedule, the majority had between twenty to thirty slaves.

In 1817, the Roanoke Navigation Company began construction on a nine-mile canal with three locks and an aqueduct that circumnavigated the falls of the Roanoke River. The company purchased African-American slaves to build the canal. They were among the eleven thousand African-American slaves enumerated in the Mecklenburg County U.S. Census of 1820. The population in Mecklenburg was 19,786 in 1820 and 674 of them were free people of color.[29]

The new State Constitution of 1902 prohibited whites and blacks from attending public schools together. It also imposed a poll or voting tax. This resulted in the number of black voters in Virginia being reduced from approximately 147 thousand to less than ten thousand by 1904. Before this, Virginia's population was

---

[29] National Register of Historic Places, Clarksville Historic District, Page 65

among the top twenty of the most populous states. Afterwards, it had the smallest body of voters in the United States. The size and status of Virginia's electorate stayed the same until the federal Voting Rights Act of 1965 and the 1966 U.S. Supreme Court decision that outlawed Virginia's imposition of the poll tax.[30]

Aqueea's dad actively participated in voter registration drives in the Clarksville area. He would attend meetings, distribute registration forms, assist people with filling out forms, explain the registration/voting/election process and became a local M.L.K. so to speak in the community. This assertive community advocacy led to his mailbox, which was at the roadside some ways from the farmhouse being shot up so badly that it was practically unusable. The farmhouse set back from the road and was visible only by looking up the power line that led to it. The electric power line path, the light line, was roughly about eight feet wide and had to be clear-cut of trees, shrubs, and undergrowth every once in a while in order to keep the wire free from becoming entangled with bushes and vines.

After dark, shots could be heard being fired up the light line. The family was not in danger because the part of the house that faced the electric line was the massive chimney at the driveway end of the house, the corridor porch, and a giant black walnut tree.

If any bullets reached the house, any damage that would have been done would have been bullets lodged into the chimney or the tree. Since the porch was open on bottom sides, a bullet would have been spent before it reached the stable or the other outer buildings surrounding it.

These acts of violence didn't deter Aqueea's dad. By day, the

---

[30] Ibid Page 69

haters conducted themselves as law-abiding citizens, some of whom were known by the black community. Their nighttime clandestine behavior was offensive to her dad, but it wasn't new to him. Having public-worked most of his adult life, he knew how to maneuver the color divide.

The homestead provided the additional protection his family needed. The driveway was not in the same place as the electric light line, but rather, about two-tenths of a mile away. It entered on the property of the white family's farm that bordered her dad's property line. The driveway was shared for several feet. Her dad's driveway then meandered across a dry stream, curved up a hill, ran past the graveyard of a former owner, and up another hill on which the homestead stood. It was wide enough for one vehicle and was tree-lined the entire length. The homestead was well se-cured, protected by a good stand of hardwoods, pastures, a pond, and crop fields. A new outer building, a machine/tool shed that her dad had built housed his tractor, farming equipment, and electrical tools.

If anyone tried to make it up the tree-lined narrow road or enter the homestead from one of the other areas leading up to the yard, her dad's hunting dogs would surely have sounded the alarm. Due to the events of the Civil Rights Movements, her dad started traveling with a handgun when he went to activist activi-ties. By the grace of God, he never had an incident.

TOBACCO

Tobacco made it possible for planters of the colonial period to have mansions, servants, and finery from all over the world, in-cluding Cinderella style chariots with matching horses and horsemen. George Washington was no different. When he ordered his carriage from Europe, he gave very specific instructions for wrapping it in order to protect it from being damaged during the voyage to Virginia. The colonists had huge lines of credit against their tobacco crops. The amount of their indebtedness meant that they needed large amounts of land to grow tobacco. George Washington had five thousand acres, comprised of five farms.

"The numerous outbuildings that surround the mansion call to mind the variety of labors that maintained this estate – kitchen, storehouse, smokehouse, washhouse, stable, coach house, overseer's quarters, ice house, greenhouse, and farther off from the house, a gristmill and even a distillery."[31]

To expedite work at the various farms, Washington split the field hands up and housed them at the particular farm they would be working. This meant that families were broken up and unless they stole away during the night to visit their family members, they would be separated for indefinite periods of time.

Raising tobacco is hard work. During the winter, women would break up new ground. They would dig up the stumps and break up the ground with hand tools. What they did on George Washington's farms was similar to what Aqueea's parents did. Her mom and dad would have a discussion at the dinner table about where they wanted to clear an area for the tobacco plant bed. The bed was generally not too far from the field where the plants would be planted.

To prepare the plant bed, her mom, dad, two brothers, and her second older sister would load axes, handsaws, chainsaws, and rakes onto the tractor-trailer and head down to the tobacco field,

---

[31] An Imperfect God: George Washington, His Slaves and the Creation of America, Wiencek, Farrar, Straus and Giroux, 2003

that was below the first tobacco barn. Having chosen a spot, the clearing would begin—cutting down trees, limb them up, which consisted of cutting branches off, and then, cutting the tree into lengths of logs that would fit into the furnace of the flue-cured tobacco barn. The logs would be loaded onto the trailer, taken to the woodpile, and stood up tepee style to dry. Surplus wood would be cut into shorter pieces, split, and thrown onto the woodpile; this wood was used in the kitchen cookstove and the wood stoves in the dining room and the two first floor rooms of the original part of the house. In cooler weather, the heat from the two first floor rooms provided enough warmth to knock the chill off the upstairs rooms.

The plant bed, once prepared, would be seeded with the tobacco seeds Aqueea's mom had saved from the previous year. Every year, a few choice plants would be allowed to seed; that is, when the tobacco was being topped, by breaking off the flowering top of a tobacco plant, these choice plants would be spared. Later in the season, after the flowers were fully-grown and the seeds had dried from being in the hot summer sun, her mom would gently break the top without dislodging the seeds. The top would then be taken to the tobacco strip-house and hung upside down for the final curing of the seeds. The seeds would be preserved in a cotton cloth and put safely away until the next year's plant bed was ready.

In his article "Children of the Fields," *Reader's Digest*, April 2015, Robert Andrew Powell gives a telling example of what the harvesting of tobacco is like; raising tobacco is hard work. In his article, he tells why children under eighteen years old say the hazards of working on tobacco farms are worth the risk.

"The kids wear long-sleeved shirts and heavy denim jeans

even though temperatures in the tobacco fields, where they work, will approach triple digits. They carry bottles of water and Gatorade in one hand and plastic garbage bags – ad hoc hazmat suits – in the other......They say the hazards are worth the risk to support their families."

Aqueea's mom, along with her six children, pretty much ran the farm while her husband worked various jobs off the farm.

A typically barn filling day, as it was called, consisted of getting up before dawn; taking care of routine chores such as milking the cows, feeding the hogs, gathering up eggs and feeding the chickens, getting a fire started in the kitchen cookstove, getting the tobacco slides ready which included hitching the family's cantankerous mule, Kit, to the slide, going to the tobacco field, and priming a couple of slide loads of ripe tobacco leaves which would be slopping wet with dew, bringing the tobacco leaves to the barn and unloading the leaves which were stacked on the tobacco bench, before breakfast was eaten. Those who had gone to the tobacco field would come to the house, wet and cold and everybody, hungry. The family would gather around the table and breakfast was eaten with gusto.

The tobacco slide was made to fit between tobacco rows, to be pulled by a mule and used for transporting tobacco from the field to the barn. The slide would have roll-down burlap curtains that were lowered when it got to the barn. The tobacco leaves would then be placed on a bench that was wide enough to hold two rows of ripe tobacco leaves and long enough to accommodate several slides of leaves.

After breakfast, Aqueea's mom would bank the fire in the cookstove so that the wood would burn more slowly. Whatever food the family would have for dinner (lunchtime), mostly a stew, would cook much like a crockpot, at a low temperate. When the family stopped work for dinner, a hot meal was ready. All her mom had to do was to make fresh hoecake biscuits and the eating could begin.

Aqueea's job was to wash the breakfast dishes and tidy up the dining room and kitchen; she would do the same when the family finished dinner. When she'd finished that she would take fresh water to those in the field, come back to the barn and begin tying the tobacco leaves that her mom would hand to her.

The tobacco stick was suspended on a horse, a two-legged wooden frame. At the top of each leg, a v-shaped cut was made to hold the tobacco stick. One leg would have two u-shaped nails in it to guide the tobacco string—one midway up the leg and the other at the top of the leg. The tobacco string was then fed through these guides and pulled to the opposite end of the tobacco stick. The string would be slipped through a notch opening at the end of the stick to secure it.

The first ripe leaves of tobacco, about three to four leaves depending on the thickness of the leaves, would be double wrapped with the string. Thereafter, the leaves would be strung down the tobacco stick to the end of it.

Keeping the leaves close to the stick and the string tight enough without it cutting through the leaves was crucial. The leaves had to be supported on the stick without hanging loose or dangling. Tying the tobacco leaves securely was important because once cured, loosely tied leaves could fall on hot flue pipes in the barn and cause a barn-burning fire. Using sturdy and straight tobacco sticks was vital too. If a weak or bent stick filled with heavy ripe leaves hanging between the rafters fell, it could cause sticks below it to fall too. In such cases, a barn could catch fire.

After a stick was filled, the string would be tied by pulling it through the notch at the end of the stick tight enough so that there was no slack in the string from the beginning of the stick to the end of it, but not so tight that the string would cut through the leaves. This, too, could result in the leaves falling on flue pipes and endangering the barn and its precious content.

The completed stick of tied, ripe tobacco leaves would then be laid on a pile near the barn door. Each subsequent stick would follow the pattern of the first layer. The pile could reach seven to eight feet high depending on how much tobacco was primed that day. At the end of the day, the sticks of tobacco would be handed up to the two people inside the barn and be hung on rafters. Each row of rafters was called a room, and the rooms were filled one at a time. A typical barn would have about six rooms of six sets of rafters about six levels high made to hold tobacco sticks. The height of the rafters was placed to accommodate tobacco leaves so that heat could flow through them for drying or curing. Once the barn was filled and ready for curing, the furnace would be filled with logs from the wood-stack. Once fired up, the heat from the flue pipes that ran around the perimeter of the barn would begin to heat it up. Temperature would be increased during the different stages of the curing process and continued uninterrupted until the leaves were cured to a golden-colored, wonderful smelling barn full of cured tobacco.

A thermometer hung from one of the rafters by the barn door was used to gauge the temperature. The wood that had been cut earlier and stacked tepee style during the winter months and early spring was now dry enough to burn evenly to provide the fuel to keep a steady climate in the barn, day and night until the tobacco leaves were properly cured. Ollie had to maintain an even temperature, which meant getting up during the night to keep watch.

After the tobacco was cured, it was taken down and transported to the tobacco pack house where it would rest until it was ready to be sorted when the markets opened. Aqueea's mom and dad would decide which of the packed tobacco they wanted to sell first, the ground, middle or top leaves. Each category had a different value. After deciding which leaves they wanted to sell, that pile would be removed from the pack house and taken to the tobacco strip house.

The tobacco, after being transported to the strip house, would be piled on the floor in the strip house when it was ready to be sorted. A number of sticks were placed in a room off the sorting floor. The leaves were lightly sprinkled with water to soften them. One stick at a time would be placed on a tobacco horse and the string that held the tobacco would be unstrung. Nothing was wasted. The used string would be tied to the end of the last used string and rolled into a ball to be used for the next year's tobacco tying. The unstrung leaves would systematically be placed on the sorting bench. While Aqueea and her siblings were in school, their mom would spend the day sorting the tobacco leaves.

Her dad had built the strip house, a log cabin type building, which had one window and one door. Inside, he'd built a bench that was about twelve feet long and just wide enough, about twelve inches, to accommodate the average length of a leaf of tobacco. Several holes were drilled into the bench and spindles about a foot and a half high were anchored into the holes. The biggest space on the bench was towards the middle. This space was where the cured tobacco leaves, once removed from the stick, would be placed for sorting. The other spaces on the bench would be where the different grade of leaves was placed. After her mom sorted the leaves, she didn't trust this to anyone else, the rest of the family would hand-tie the leaves, keeping the various grades separated.

Hand-tying the cured leaves consisted of gathering a group of leaves together in one hand, squeezing them tightly, then taking one leaf, folding the outer part of the leaf inward towards the stem which ran down the middle of the leaf, and folding the outer edge again to form a wrap of about an inch wide. Using the top part of the leaf wrap, the bundle of leaves would be wrapped tightly. Starting at the top of the bundle, the leaf wrapper is wrapped to form a cap, which covers the stems of the leaves in the bundle.

The bundle then is wrapped down to about three to four inches from the top. The end of the wrap is poked through the middle of the bundle so that the leaves in the bundle are fastened. The hand-tied bundles would be packed along a wall in the strip house. At the end of the day, the bundles would be hung on a smooth tobacco stick that had been sanded to remove splinters so that they could easily slide off the sticks into baskets at the tobacco warehouse.

The sticks of hand-tied tobacco would be piled on the floor of the strip house and covered. Ollie would begin scouting the markets to see what was selling. When he found a market that was buying at a good price, he would rush home, freshen up the waiting sticks of hand-tied tobacco, load it up, and take it to the market to be sold.

The cash crop—tobacco—the major cash reward at one time was the major amount of money that came in for the year and paid for the farm expenses: schoolbooks and fees, taxes, shoes and clothes and all the basic needs for the farm and the family. Aqueea's dad's public-work paid almost nothing in comparison to what the tobacco crop paid. His jobs only took care of the day-to-day minor needs of the farm and the family, but tobacco, though labor intensive, was the life-blood the family relied on to secure independence. Though raising tobacco was labor intensive, it was the family's financial life-blood.

Ollie wasn't wealthy, but tobacco paid for his farm. There were those, however, who did become wealthy. Tobacco made George Washington, the Skipwith family, (Prestwould Plantation) of Mecklenburg County, Virginia, through their slaves, and all colonial planters wealthy. Virginia produced more tobacco and had more slaves than any of the other colonies.

In 1772, George Washington wrote a purchase order for slaves specifying that all of them needed to be straight and limber, strong and pleasant to look at, with good teeth and that the males be twenty years old and the females, sixteen years old.[32]

Washington, in all probability, was growing "laborers as if they were a crop," as Wiencek suggested, since the number of his taxable slaves increased from 49 to 135 within fourteen years.

Farm life for Aqueea and her family, she discovered, was much like farm life in colonial times on George Washington's farms. The way her parents ran the farm led her to conclude that her

[32] Ibid, page 126

ancestor more than likely was of the field slave division based on her readings.

According to Wiencek, "sixty-five percent of the working field slaves were women, and Washington was demanding and punctilious in his instructions for them. He wrote to a manager:

'when I say grub well I mean that everything wh. is not to remain as trees should be taken up by the roots; ... that the Plow may meet with no interruption, and the field lye perfectly smooth for the Scythe.'"[33]

Twenty-eight percent of the slave force consisted of these skilled laborers, seventy-five percent of whom were men; this force included mulattos.[34]

Seventy-five percent of the laborers were field hands in the following areas:

- Hoeing
- Ploughing [plowing]
- Harvesting
- Building fences

Sixty-one percent of the field hands were women; field hands lived on the outlying farms.[35]

Andrew Carnegie said, "The secret of success lies not in doing your work, but in recognizing the right man to do it." For a certainty, the colonial planters quickly learned that more tobacco needed more land and more land needed more slaves.

The set up at Mount Vernon mirrored a colonial plantation

---

[33] Ibid, page 98

[34] George Washington's Mount Vernon, http://www.mountvernon.org

[35] Ibid.

in Clarksville, Mecklenburg County, Virginia. The plantation was not far from Aqueea's family's farm. The Prestwould Plantation was owned by Sir Peyton Skipwith who was originally from England built the Prestwould house in 1794. He made his fortune from tobacco. Among his skilled slaves were wagoners, weavers, and woodsmen. His slave house was a single room structure measuring roughly twelve feet by sixteen feet.[36]

Prestwould was the largest plantation in the state. A number of the original outbuildings and the garden of Lady Jean, his wife, are now tourist attractions. Papers and records of the Skipwith family provide insight into slave deeds, lists, and sales agreements of enslaved individuals. Humberton Skipwith, their son, had 247 slaves.

The high school Aqueea graduated from (1954–1958) is located in the unincorporated community of Skipwith, Virginia, so named in commemoration of the Skipwith family. The high school, though still located in Skipwith, and the same structure Aqueea attended which was for the colored children who lived in the west end of the county, after schools were integrated, was renamed Bluestone Jr. High School to commemorate William Byrd II. In the 1700s, he built a hunting lodge in Mecklenburg County and named it Bluestone Castle. There was nothing to commemorate blacks.

Byrd was concerned about how slavery created a mindset in whites that they were above doing work because they felt it was beneath them. He also found that white workers at the lower level were strenuously conscious of any act that might be looked upon as equating them to the level of a slave's standing—food,

---

[36] Prestwould Plantation, http://www.aahistoricsitesva.org

clothing, lodging or whatever. The wealthy took on the behavior of European royalty. They had the benefits, generated from the work division of slaves, to have every aspect of living as did a person of royal standing abroad. The only things missing were the official titles, the accompanying pomp and circumstance surrounding those European titles, and the societal acknowledgements that went with these titles. The colonist did, however, call themselves gentlemen and gentlewomen, a term applied to the owners of large plantations such as George Washington, his peers, and their wives.

The slave system was so embedded in Virginia, that according to Wiencek, a minister wrote that help such as poor whites and free blacks, couldn't be hired which resulted in more slaves being purchased. Wiencek's research set forth the following statistics relating to the slave population in Virginia:

- 13,000 in 1700
- 40,000 in 1730
- 105,000 in 1750, approximate eighty percent Virginia-born

The colonial period is deeply woven into the fabric of current day Mecklenburg County, Virginia. Aqueea found that the largest slave population in the state was in Mecklenburg County. As she did her chain of deeds search, she recognized the surnames of families in the community—descendants of colonial farmers, most of who were slave owners. The presence of colonial surnames on buildings and artifacts, Aqueea realized, helped to keep the colonial legacy of those families alive with their current day descendants. She found that William Byrd, II, who named Buffalo Springs, Virginia that was located less than five miles west of her home, was a distant relative of George Washington through marriage.

Mecklenburg County citizens, characterized as being frontier at the time of the Revolutionary War, paid war taxes of beef on the hoof. If cattle weighed more than three hundred pounds, a certificate was issued to the farmer that was a public claim against the government for later payment. Certificates were issued for horses, guns, and other items too. Taxes were also collected in the form of grains, tobacco, pork, and other produce.

Transportation was by horse, wagon, carriage or boat in the colonial period. The roads were dirt and when it had rained, became muddy and in some areas, unusable. William Royster acquired land in the area known as Mecklenburg County in 1752, which resulted in the 1750s remote outpost becoming more settled. Royster established a ferry, built a lodge, and began to make food and lodging available for customers who used his ferry service. Later, one hundred acres of his land was made into the town Clarksville named after his son, Clarke. The town, Clarksville became incorporated in 1818.

BLACKS IN UNIFORMS

When George Washington got to New England, he found blacks carrying guns and were enlisted and accepted in Minute Men units. Blacks had fought and fought nobly. In the first months of the war in Massachusetts, blacks had spontaneously joined the patriot cause; left to itself, the army had integrated spontaneously. Change was occurring on its own without a formal policy imposing or urging it. The natural movement was toward freedom. Washington and other leaders would have to act to stifle this movement.[37]

Blacks were present in every aspect of the Revolutionary War either as free blacks or slaves at the side of their masters as was Billy Lee to George Washington. Or they were spies as was James Armistead who was returned to slavery in spite of the service he provided to America or they were present as the men of the First Rhode Island Regiment. Washington, as Commander-In-Chief of the Continental Army, seeing the discipline and skill of blacks in arms for freedom, could have championed emancipation. However, his peers such as Thomas Jefferson and his elitist associates who took the position that blacks were inferior to whites influenced Washington to uphold the slavery system that was so firmly established in Virginia and the south in general. Blacks who fought in the battle at Bunker Hill fought so bravely that one of them, Peter Salem, was introduced to Washington. His bravery was never written down in history. The black men at Bunker Hill and other aspects of bravery have never had their stories told; they've never been heralded for their heroism, and the government has never issued them a certificate of payment for service.

ON LITERACY

George Washington, when he received a communication from Phillis Wheatley, was speechless. As Wiencek put it, "...December 1775 was a month of startling revelations: black men demanding a place in his army; a black woman sending him a poem."[38]

---

[37] Wiencek, page 199

[38] Ibid, page 206

In Virginia, Washington and his peers saw to it that white orphans and bastards were taught reading, writing, and a useful trade; mulatto children were not taught anything. They were routed to the lowest rung of the laboring class.[39]

It was against the law to teach slaves how to read and write, but they were taught skills such as gardening, construction, and fence building. Though mulattoes were placed at the bottom of the laboring class, Wiencek notes that Washington surrounded himself with them but sent dark-skinned slaves to the fields.

Aqueea reflected on the ways in which the Virginia planters methodically imposed the noose around the lives of blacks. This noose was drawn so tightly that even colonists who may have had favored emancipation of the enslaved feared to raise their voices.

At the same time these planters were restricting the education and empowerment of blacks, they were busy educating their sons. As Wiencek pointed out, from the time of George Washington's great-great grandfather, John Washington, a shipmate who could read and write, after marrying the daughter of Nathaniel Pope, an illiterate but wealthy Virginian, paved the way for the Washington family to gain access to the elite circle of colonists and English officials, the family maintained prominent positions in government from then on, generation to generation.

George Washington didn't get the opportunity to go abroad to study in England as his two older half-brothers did because of the death of his father. At the age of eleven, he started his own educational pursuit of becoming self-taught. Washington trained himself to live by the book, or more accurately, by three books *The Rules of Civility*, Seneca's *Morals* and Joseph Addison's tragedy *Cato*.

---

[39] Ibid, page 129

A question Aqueea would ask each new class of her students throughout her more than thirty years of teaching was "What do you want to be?" It was disturbing to her that only a handful of students, adults or teens, were able to answer the question. One of the things that the colonists did was teach their sons the function of government and plantation management, which George Washington had been schooled in from his early teens.

To help her students think about what they could become, Aqueea would give them a values clarification exercise to complete. The activity started with students ranking a number of items from lowest to highest in terms of importance to them. She'd been exposed to this exercise herself when she attended a values clarification workshop for teachers. Education was one of the items on the list. When the presenter asked participants to share their ranking choices, Aqueea and one other participant, a person of color, had ranked education as number one. During the discussion, the other participants asked Aqueea and the other minority why they'd put education as their first choice because for them, education was a given. It was understood that in their culture, education was fundamental.

In her earlier years of teaching adults, Aqueea had seen the drive in them for completing their secondary education. However, just before she was assigned to teach high school students, she found that students in the adult education program were younger and more disruptive. These students were former alternative high school students who had aged out and enrolled in the adult education program. The older adults complained about the younger students' distracting behavior in class. The students in the alternative high school program had more of an "I don't care" attitude; they were in school because they were under the age of sixteen and had to be in school by law. Completing their secondary education wasn't looked upon as a rite of passage.

The exercise she had her students complete after ranking their values clarification list was to write a statement of their philosophy of life, something that guided their actions and way of thinking. She used Benjamin Franklin's quote: "What I am to be, I am now becoming" as a thought for the students to consider. Next, she'd ask them to write a motto that made a statement about them. She found that most of her students had not thought about who they were or where they were going. Many of them, unknowingly, were following a self-perpetuating culture that Richard Stengel wrote about in an article for *Time Magazine*[40] in which he described the Seven Ages of Underclass Man and Woman. Stengel labeled this group as those who live without. He stated that they were prisoners of a ghetto pathology, "… denizens characterized by teenage pregnancy, fatherless households, chronic unemployment, crime, drug use and long-term dependence on welfare." The new term for labeling this population in the twenty-first century is the Pipeline to Prison or School to Prison generation. Aqueea saw a mentality among her students that encouraged them to gravitate towards that funnel. Committing crimes and serving time in the youth house was seen, as a badge of honor among males and becoming pregnant was a way females used to get their own apartments using public assistance.

When Aqueea would give the Stengel article to her students to read, she asked them to write the date they thought it was written; she found that they, in every instance, used the date on which

---

[40] The Underclass: Breaking the Cycle, Time, October 10, 1988

it was read. They had no idea of how long ago the article had been written because they felt it accurately described current events.

How effectively the planter's noose has clung to the minds of the enslaved and their descendants. Generational inhibitors, their breeding and selling of blacks and the disregard for family unity bred a feeling of inhibitions, indifference, classicism, lack of solidarity in the black community that has impaired its ability to rise above the whites' oppressiveness. The planters' slave codes have had the effect as the chain around the baby elephant's leg. As a baby, the elephant found that it could go no further than the chain around its leg. As an adult, it stopped trying to break loose when it went as far as the chain was long, even though it had the strength to not only break the chain but to uproot the stake as well. Each day the American black community has to deal with those chains—chains founded and established by the Backcountry-England-Bourgeois mentality, the status quo class.

When the planters stopped importing slaves and began to breed their own, they broke the link to the Mother Land that had sustained many of those enslaved who remembered that they were kings, queens, and leaders in their tribes. Over time, the Mother Land was forgotten. After decades of being sold, running away, and being placed into a caste system, their past was forgotten.

Dr. Arnold Lockett wrote: "Unless there is contrary data, black Americans (North, Central, and South) are the only people on earth who cannot say from which country they came. The only thing they know is that their ancestral roots are somewhere on the African continent." [41]

---

[41] Lockett, Dr. Arnold, Stolen Identities, Where are the lost African Tribes? 2004

The planters' slave practices became an institution that has become embedded in black culture.

"However laudable an ambition to rise may be, the first duty of an upper class is to serve the lowest classes. The aristocracies of all people have been slow in learning this, and perhaps the Negro is no slower than the rest, but his peculiar situation demands that in his case this lesson be learned sooner." —William E. B. DuBois, The Philadelphia Negro, 1899[42]

According to Majors, at least four hundred million blacks in the south, in 1870, were illiterate; they could neither read nor write and had never been in a classroom, much less having had a book in their hands. The Southern planters used this to their advantage. They knew the ins and outs of government and had networks of power brokers at their disposal to regain their broken, but not lost, society. As archaeologists would tape together pieces of artifacts from long ago to bring to life a vessel from another era, so did the whites from their dismantled southern way of life. While supportive whites and blacks from the north went south at the end of the Civil War to help the newly freed slaves, carpetbaggers and other opportunists took advantage of the ignorance of this group.

Empire of the Owls,[43] by H. V. Traywick, gives an account of "Reflections on the North's War against Southern secession." One such reflection was written of Lt. Gen. Richard Taylor, from Destruction and Reconstruction: "In their dealings with the negro the white men of the South should ever remember that no instance of outrage occurred during the war. Their wives and little ones remained safe at home, surrounded by thousands of

---

[42] Majors, Geraldyn, Black Society, Johnson Publishing Company, Inc., 1976
[43] Traywick, Jr., H.V., Empire of the Owls, Dementi Milestone Publishing, 2013

faithful slaves, who worked quietly in the fields until removed by the Federals."

A wave of sorrow swept over Aqueea. She was saddened by the underlying, unspoken impact that decades of enslavement had created in the field slaves referred to in Taylor's writing. These people, like the chained elephant, had become conditioned to their plight. Her sadness was as much for the high school students she'd taught in the twenty-first century as it was for those wretched souls of the eighteenth, nineteenth and twentieth century. Freedom, education, and independence were just words to the field hands; they had no concept of the power and empowerment those words could bring to them if they were literate. They didn't know what the Constitution was and the promise it held for them. Like them, many current day students, not just blacks, have acquired an apathetical attitude about the history of the United States. Sadly, the struggle of blacks in America is unknown by many immigrants of the Diaspora.

James Oppenheim wrote the following poem:

The Slave
They set the slave free, striking off his chains...
Then he was as much of a slave as ever.
He was still chained to servility,
He was still manacled to indolence and sloth,
He was still bound by fear and superstition,
By ignorance, suspicion, and savagery...
His slavery was not in the chains,
But in himself...
They can only set free men free...

And there is no need of that:
Free men set themselves free.

What both Taylor and Oppenheim failed to acknowledge was the state of the enslaved blacks. For example, George Washington, in his records, noted how shabby the slaves' clothing was, yet, according to Wiencek, he gave his slaves clothing only once a year.

The field slaves were the most piteous because they were at the bottom of the work force and most likely to be the first to be overlooked and abused. Planters tended to put the darkest skinned, curly haired slaves the farthest from the manor house. The pleasant looking ones, who were often mulattoes, worked in and around the manor. These slaves, since they were fairly close to the slave owners' day-to-day life, learned social graces and some even secretly learned to read and write.

Aqueea thought about the words in Oppenheim's poem. *If slaves got clothes once a year with no replacements for garments that had been outgrown or damaged, how could they not look slovenly, nasty, raggedy, and dirty?* she said to herself. "Not only that," she said aloud, "How could the masses benefit from the freedom that the Civil Rights Act of 1866 gave them if they'd never left the plantation, or held a book in their hands?" In her mind's eye, she imagined the federalist running out to the fields screaming at the slaves, "Drop your plow! Throw down that sickle, now! You've got to leave! You are free!"

She reasoned that the women would huddle together as they walked, ran, and scurried towards the slave outbuilding—the only place they knew—where they'd lived.

"Get your stuff and keep walking!" the federalist on horseback probably shouted to the scared slaves as they inched toward the shanty near the fields they tended, the place they called home. Nobody had told them about freedom. They wondered what they were supposed to do with it. What would master say about them walking off, better yet, driven off the plantation by these strangers on horseback? Where would they sleep? Who would give them food? Would they be caught as a runaway? Beaten? For some, this was the first time they had ever left the plantation.

How could the masses understand or appreciate freedom? The slave owners had bred decades of laborers who only knew the field; they were field hands. The fact that the federalist drove them off the plantations suggests that they didn't know where to go or what to do. As a result, many of them found their way back to the plantation and worked as hired laborers or became sharecroppers. Those who were able to assert themselves were met with strong resistance.

Booker T. Washington gave a vivid interpretation of the newly freed slave. "The great responsibility of being free, of having charge of themselves, of having to think and plan for themselves and their children, seemed to take possession of them. It was very much like suddenly turning a youth of ten or twelve years out into the world to provide for himself."[44]

Former slaves who had a voice soon found that their claims for forty acres and a mule fell on deaf ears. They were refused land purchases from whites and the federal government didn't redistribute land in the south to them to help

---

[44] Washington, Booker T., Up from Slavery: An Autobiography, Doubleday, Page, & Co., NY, 1901

them get started on the road to being independent. Nonetheless, it restored property to whites who put in claims for property taken or lost, including compensation for slaves who'd been chased off the plantations.

In an effort to promote supporters for policies put in place by the Lincoln administration, blacks created Union leagues. These leagues espoused loyalty to the Union, and the Republican Party. Members of the leagues met secretly and sought to mobilize workers to oppose certain employers whom they thought were enemies of the new ways of the south. There were those who indeed were against the new regime. "The poor whites never laid aside their hostility towards the blacks, bond or free."[45]

"The influence of the league over the Negro was due in large degree to the mysterious secrecy of the meetings, the weird imitation ceremony that made him feel fearfully good from his head to his heel, the imposing ritual, and the songs. The ritual, it is said, was not used in the north; it was probably adopted for the particular benefit of the African. The would-be leaguer was informed that the emblems of the order were the altar, the Bible, the Declaration of Independence, the Constitution of the United States, the flag of the Union, censer, sword, gavel, ballot box, sickle, shuttle, anvil, and other emblems of industry. He was told to the accompaniment of clanking chains and groans that the objects of the order were to preserve liberty, to perpetuate the Union, to maintain the laws of the Constitution, to secure the ascendancy of American institutions, to protect, defend, and strengthen all loyal men and members of the Union League in all rights of person and property, to demand the elevation of

---

[45] Traywick, page 315

labor, to aid in the education of laboring men, and to teach the duties of American citizenship."[46]

Traywick indicates, "some of the methods of the Loyal League were similar to those of the later Ku Klux Klan."[47] The Reconstruction Acts of March 1867 opened the door for blacks to enter the political arena, but their lack of education, economics, and government made them prime targets of northerners who manipulated them and the elections. The blacks who were the most successful during this period were those who…

> "had gained their freedom before the Civil War (by self-purchase or through the will of a deceased owner), worked as a skilled slave artisan, served in the Union Army"[48]

Many black political leaders came from churches, one of the places where blacks could congregate before and after the Emancipation Proclamation.

THE THIRD EMANCIPATION: A NEW PEOPLE — A NEW CLAN

The third emancipation is on the horizon, even at the door. America has gone through many passages, but never to the passage of reckoning with the wrongs it has done to survivors of the Middle Passage and their descendants. Georgetown University, Washington, DC and Rutgers University, New Jersey have taken some small steps towards acknowledging their role in utilizing slave labor in the construction of buildings. Their efforts are very

---

[46] Ibid, page 312

[47] Ibid, page 315

[48] www.history.com/topics/american- civil- war/black- leaders- during- Reconstruction

small steps for giving credit to the genius and contributions of blacks. Thomas Jefferson's contrived philosophy of racial prejudice still permeates the minds of whites and is their bulwark for perpetrating racial divides in America. Each time milestones are made in advancing the country towards the Constitution's Preamble that all men are created equal, the Backcountry-England-Bourgeois mentality vanguard brings out its clandestine networks of interconnected systems of controls. It uses economics, politics, and demographics to reinforce and sustain the status quo control of the American schemata. The Backcountry-England-Bourgeois mentality of the ruling class and the backcountry-frontier mentality of the poor whites of the 1700s ignite in the hearts and minds of this group's modern-day descendants. They put into action the words of Thomas Jefferson written to Edward Coles in 1814... and this mindset is fixed in the sociological and psychological orientation of this class.

The first emancipation could have happened during the Revolutionary War when free blacks, without hesitation, took up arms to defend the country. It could have happened when both black and white indentured servants, worked together, associated together, and in some instances lived together as a family. The Emancipation Proclamation was signed to end slavery in slave states, but the practices of treating blacks as less than human beings didn't stop. When Aqueea read that Abraham Lincoln deliberated colonization for freed slaves and had cost out their deportation outside of the United States, she saw clearly that America had no intentions of embracing blacks or compensating them for having been exploited. After such a long time as slaves, and many of them were bred in America which was a practice of slave owners, including George Washington, more than likely, the Mother Land instinct had been bred out of them for the most part, and they became domesticated, living androids. The American society and the American culture was all they knew, Aqueea reasoned, but they were shadows that fell on the daily day-to-day life of their surroundings. They couldn't take the form of matter because they had no physical substance; their existence was nonexistence. She remembered the scene in an ESL workshop she'd attended. English-as-a-Second-Language (ESL) teachers in the northeast section of the country had been assigned to attend a series of mental health workshops for ESL students to help ESL teachers to better deal with the socio-emotional stress of immigrants. As an icebreaker activity the first day of four subsequent sessions, each workshop participant had been given a thumbtack as they entered the room. Placing her thumbtack on the desk after she'd walked in, Aqueea looked around the room. There were artifacts from around the world on the teacher's desk: nested Russian dolls, a Chinese Rickshaw, a statue of a matador and charging bull. Then she turned her attention to the large world map that was mounted in front of the classroom on a corkboard; she contemplated what cities the souvenirs had come from.

"Teachers, when they get together, tend to be noisy," she said to a participant who had come in and taken a seat across from her as she introduced herself. There was a din in the hallway just outside of the classroom. People who knew each other from other workshops were busy greeting one another and trading district woes and classroom challenges. Almost as soon as Aqueea had introduced herself to the other teacher, the workshop facilitator went to the door and asked everybody to come in and get seated. She asked if everyone had gotten a thumbtack and as an aide gave a thumbtack to those who didn't, the instructor explained the purpose of the workshop. Thereafter, she said, "Each of you is to come to the map and place your thumbtack on the map. Then I'd like you to tell a little about yourself and why you placed your thumbtack where you did."

The teachers dutifully came to the front placing their thumbtacks on different areas of the world.

"I placed my thumbtack on Italy because my grandparents came through Ellis Island from Sicily," one teacher said.

"I placed mine on Ireland," another said, because my great-great-great grandparents came from Ulster." So it went until only two people were left, Aqueea and another teacher of color. Aqueea smiled at her and beckoned for her to go first.

The teacher strutted to the map, pushed in her thumbtack and exclaimed, "I'm from North Carolina. My parents, grandparents, uncles and aunts, cousins, all of us are from North Carolina; we are North Carolinians." As had been done for the other teachers, she was given a round of applause. All eyes now focused on Aqueea. She moved with purpose, to the front of the room. She stood at the edge of the map and moved her hand over the continent of Africa. With her finger, she outlined the Congo.

"Here?" she asked, looking out onto the faces of the participants. She paused, then turning back to the map; with her finger, she traced the shape of Nigeria. "Aw, maybe here?" she queried. "Or here, from Burkina Faso, or maybe Cote D'Ivoire, or Togo, or Benin, or Ghana?" She had a contemplative look on her face.

Smiling at the teachers and stepping back from the map, she took a deep breath. Straightening her shoulders back, she put one hand over the other in front of her, as she bent her elbows, bringing her arms close to her side. "I've had students from each of the countries I've mentioned as well as from Kenya, Egypt, Iran, Iraq, Israel, Russia, Brazil, Peru… in other words, I've had students from all over the world in my classroom." She waved her thumb-tack over the map as if it were a magic wand; then she stuck it on the west coast of Africa. In an authoritative voice she said, "Of all the students who've come to my classroom, there has not been one of them who could not tell about their ancestry. I placed my thumbtack on West Africa because of the Middle Passage, the in-famous slave trade," and pointing to her face, she concluded with, "and the color of my skin."

All of a sudden, she felt the childhood specter that had haunted her so long with the question "Who am I?" beginning to release its query. The light of her roots began to illuminate in her mind. "I appreciate what my colleague from North Carolina said about being a North Carolinian," Aqueea said as she nodded her head in the direction of the North Carolinian teacher. "Given the fact that I know nothing about my ancestor, what people of Africa he or she was from, if he was a tribal chief or she a queen mother, the language he or she spoke, by the way, there are hun-dreds of languages spoken in Africa, what culture he or she prac-ticed… since my African heritage has been stripped away and replaced with Americanism, I am an American-African, a Virgin-ian American-African."

As she returned to her seat, one of the participants exploded with a loud "Wow!" The room broke into an ear-deafening round of applause as she took her seat, for they understood what the institution of slavery had and has done to American blacks.

From that time forward, the pieces of the "Who am I?" jigsaw puzzle started coming into focus. Each piece brought into focus a sharper view in her mind's eye of her ancestors' journeys. The specter of that unknown loved one who came to Aqueea that November day when her little sister was born had driven her to this moment so that she could begin to learn of her heritage firsthand from immigrant Africans she'd be meeting in the not so far distance—things, things that weren't in textbooks.

Aqueea understood the sacrifices her parents had made in buying the farm and loved them for creating a safety zone, the place for the family where not only she, but her siblings as well, could grow up less scathed by segregation. It was a place where they could run, play, and work without racial slurs and harassment by hostile whites. As an adult, each summer when her two children were out of school, she would head to the farm so they could have the same experiences she'd had as a child. They would always stay on the farm, helping out where they could, until it was time to go back north to get ready for school. Attitudes had changed in Mecklenburg County to some extent. For example, her nieces and nephews had attended integrated schools and her dad and Baby Sista had driven school bus loads of black and white children to and from school. A new generation had been born, but the ruling class still had control. Blacks were buying homes, opening businesses, and getting jobs in fields never before available to them such as in law-enforcement and becoming active in politics. Aqueea called this phenomenon the third emancipation. While the country was nowhere near where it needed to be in terms of being equitable to all people, at least here in her little backcountry-frontier county, doors were being opened. She recognized that her sons and their generation's thinking patterns were new. While control of economics, politics, and government remained with the Backcountry-England-Bourgeois mentality class and the backcountry-frontier mentality class still had its hostilities towards black, at least education had opened up so that blacks and minorities could learn skills, vocational trades or become professionals.

After considering how her ancestry had been systematically dismantled and not knowing her African clan, she wondered if American-Africans would buy into creating a new clan. This new clan would be representative of survivors of the Middle Passage and descendants of the slaves from the colonial era in America. She started formulating in her mind an artifact that she would create to serve as a reminder to her posterity what the Middle Passage was and what it means to be a Birthright American.

THE RECONSTRUCTION PERIOD

The Reconstruction Period provided some blacks with opportunities, but whites continued to destroy a great deal of what had been accomplished by them. For example, the land that General Sherman had ordered for blacks was taken back and given to whites when President Andrew Johnson took office following the death of Abraham Lincoln. It seemed that when the black community made one step forward, it was pushed back two. The resilience of the black race can, however, be epitomized in the following poem:

The Negro Speaks of Rivers

I've known rivers;

I've known rivers ancient as the world and older than the flow of human

blood in human veins.

My soul has grown deep like the rivers.

I bathed in the Euphrates when dawns were young.

I built my hut near the Congo and it lulled me to sleep.

I looked upon the Nile and raised the pyramids above it.

I heard the singing of the Mississippi when Abe Lincoln went down to New

Orleans, and I've seen its muddy bosom turn all golden in the sunset.

I've known rivers:

Ancient, dusky rivers.

My soul has grown deep like the rivers

                         Langston Hughes, 1902 – 1967

The Civil War created a lot of anxieties for the newly freed slave. All of a sudden, thousands of blacks were thrust from the boiling pot of slavery and propelled in the fire of survival without any mentoring on how to sustain themselves and without any land on which they could foray. For them there was no Statue of Liberty crying out, "Bring to me your huddled masses yearning to breathe free." They only had each other, herded together as a flock without a shepherd. However, their souls, having grown deep like the river, moved them to take on the feeling of freedom, the first of which was to name themselves.

Aqueea made a trip to a terminal in Jersey City, New Jersey to examine the census records of 1850 to research her family's surname. Looking at the current day general geographical area her family lived, she found that her surname belonged to white slave owners; two of her sisters, an uncle, and a cousin had the first names of that family of slave owners and her dad had both the first and surname of a man. Her brother, who was named after their dad, always had a good laugh when he told about when the police once stopped him for a traffic infraction. Looking at his credentials, they were about to arrest him because his name is the same as that of a well-known actor. She further learned that her little sister's name was that of an unmarried white woman, age fifty-seven, who owned three black males, ages forty, twenty-three, and ten; and eight black females, ages thirty-eight, twenty-one, nineteen, fourteen, thirteen, eight, six and six, and the man after whom her dad was named owned fifteen slaves; eight black males, ages thirty-two, twenty-one, eighteen, sixteen, sixteen, eleven, seven, and seven black females, ages fifty-four, thirty-four, eighteen, thirteen, eight, five, and two.[49] When she did her chain of deed search at the County Seat in Boydton, Virginia, she found no evidence of her dad's family's surname in those records and there was no one in the area with that name either. After not finding any leads to discovering her roots using her dad's surname, she thought about an incident involving a giant oak tree, one of the longest living plants on earth, that occurred outside her classroom window.

---

[49] County Spine District, Page 983, Nov. 29, 1850, Census Record, Abrahams Planes Dist., Dec. 14, 1850

The Oak Tree

After correcting and posting her students' work, Aqueea went to her desk. Taking a seat, she leaned back in the squeaky, old-fashioned oak chair; its wheels were badly in need of replacement. A new or at least a newer chair was needed.

She was alone in her classroom because she made a habit of coming to work early. She liked getting to her classroom about half an hour or so before her students arrived. She enjoyed the quiet time to reflect on the day's agenda, critique her lesson plan, think about the direction she wanted to take the students, and how best to do it. These students were old enough to be signed out of school but were trying to get their GED diploma to finish their secondary education. They were neither the easiest students to teach nor the most motivated to learn. They were in class in the mornings and on job sites in the afternoon where they practiced the employability skills taught in class, unlike the Alternative High School students she would be teaching years later who followed the regular school day calendar.

Construction work going on outside, not far from her classroom window, caught her attention.

"They're really noisy today," she said to herself as she walked to the window to get a better view of what was going on. Indeed the construction crew was busy. They were engaged in cutting down a huge oak tree, the trunk of which was easily three feet in diameter.

"If I'm not mistaken," she whispered to herself, "there are roughly 450 different types of oak trees; I wonder if that tree is an English oak, which can live for nine hundred years... I remember that tree."

The tree grew on the campus of the small college where Aqueea did her undergraduate studies. The college was well known for its superior academic program. It was ranked tenth among small private institutions of learning in the country for its rigorous programs of study. While a student there, Aqueea had struggled working full time, attending classes in the evenings, on week-ends, and during summer, while at the same time being a mom and a wife; but she completed her studies graduating with a bachelor's degree, earning a major in sociology and a minor in psychology. She'd continued on to graduate school earning a master's of arts in teaching, becoming certified as a teacher of English.

She didn't stop there. She enrolled in post-graduate studies and became certified as a teacher of English-as-a-Second-Language (ESL).

She reminisced, as she took in the scene outside her classroom window. This same classroom where she now taught delinquent teens, had been where she'd taken numerous under-graduate classes in the past.

"I never thought that my alma mater would have come to this," Aqueea said aloud. "The manicured lawns, gone. The ornamental Japanese trees that I loved so much, gone. The library, a beautiful structure, now in disrepair. What happened to this pristine institution of beauty?" She knew the answer. Not only was the college ranked among the top ten small private colleges in the country, but the city was too. The city itself was as pristine as the college then, with up-scale department stores on the avenue and streets safe to walk day or night. However, like many other cities and institutions, after the riots and social unrest across the country during the sixties, white flight left blight, empty office buildings and high-rise luxury apartments with depilated insides were vacant.

Aqueea thought of the July morning in 1967 when her husband, an insurance salesman, had dropped her off at a department store that was about ten blocks from his office in the downtown area of the city that bordered where they lived. The insurance agency was near city hall, so her husband had taken her downtown so she could do some shopping while his mother watched their six-month-old infant son and his almost three-year-old brother. They hadn't heard about the rioting that had broken out downtown. In minutes her husband was back at the department store to pick her up. He couldn't get to his office—buildings were on fire; stores were being looted, and the streets had been blocked off. The downtown area fell victim to decay and so did their city following the destruction caused by the riots.

After the city purchased a portion of the college campus, the program Aqueea worked for, as well as some other classes, was temporarily housed in the building where Aqueea's classroom now was.

Her thoughts, drawn back to the construction crew, focused on the tree being cut.

"I wonder what that tree would say if it could tell its story," Aqueea murmured. "How many birds built nests in your canopy? How many squirrels have hidden your acorns some place forgotten about, that have grown into trees? When students rested on the ground beneath your shade, did they think to look up at your leaves and say, 'Thanks for the breeze?' How many gardeners have taken care of you? How many storms have rocked your limbs and broken off branches?"

As she enumerated the unheard questions to the tree, the men went about sawing sections of its trunk into logs and splitting them into two or three pieces. A crane picked up the split-up logs in its steel jaws and dropped them onto the trailer bed of an eighteen-wheeler. In the span of a few minutes, the split logs filled the trailer's bed. Twigs and small branches were mulched and the chips were blown into the bed of a dump truck while the larger branches were de-stemmed and loaded with the split logs. Before the bell rang, the eighteen-wheeler, straining with the weight of the dismembered tree, was soon out of sight. Nothing of the tree was left but the stump.

Aqueea walked back to her desk; sitting down, she looked at the classroom clock that hung above the whiteboard. She'd had it placed there because a frequent question from students was "What time is it?" The whiteboard was placed under the clock so students could follow the time and better manage their time spent on tasks. Time management, the learning objective for the day, and time on task, evaluating outcomes, and students sharing their outcomes were paramount behaviors Aqueea wanted to cultivate in her students.

She double-checked the learning objective for the day. "Do I have the three-part learning objective correctly written? Is it relevant to what I am teaching? Is the Core Content Curriculum Standard written? Is my evaluation of students learning consistent with the teaching? Have I scaffold for multiple levels in my plans... Is my Do Now easy enough that students can come in, get their journals and begin writing independently? Humm—"

She jumped when a loud noise outside interrupted her self-check. Hurriedly, she walked back to the window. Looking out, she saw a bulldozer being off-loaded from the flat bed trailer of another eighteen-wheeler.

Aqueea had a thing for eighteen-wheelers. She liked hearing the roar of their engines on the open road. Her favorites were the shiny clean ones that had matching tractor and trailer, polished to a mirror shine with exhaust pipes on both sides of the tractor. She remembered when she was a kid that she and all the other kids when they saw one coming down the highway would pump their arms hoping the driver would blast the air horn. If a trucker did, the children would dance with glee. Though she was intrigued with eighteen-wheelers, an incident happened that almost changed her mind about liking them.

Living in the country with nothing but farms, kids who lived on nearby farms would walk to and from school together. Buses hadn't started picking school children up yet. Those who lived nearer to the school waited for those like Aqueea's siblings who lived farther away. Being the youngest child in the group, Aqueea entertained herself with her books, as usual, as the other kids played around joking and teasing each other. Their horsing around didn't distract her. She would be oblivious to her surroundings.

One day, she was completely engrossed in a book as she walked down the middle of the narrow asphalt roadway. It wasn't unusual for the children to take over the road because traffic was seldom on it and therefore, they were the traffic, except for this day.

While the children were playing around, they saw an eighteen-wheeler approaching and all of them immediately got to both sides of the road and waited for it to reach them all but Aqueea, that is. She was so engrossed in her book that she heard nothing and saw nothing.

The children silently waited to see what would happen and she read on. Seeing that she wasn't going to get out of the road, the children started yelling at her, "Get out of the road!" Their shouts broke through her fantasy—the journey where her book had taken her—but she thought the children were playing a trick on her and quickly let her imagination take her back to pick up on her journey in the book. By then, the eighteen-wheeler was right on her. Unaware of what was going on, she continued her walk, right down the middle of the road. The trucker had come to a complete stop. Absorbed in her book, Aqueea was not yielding to traffic.

Finally, the children began to pump their arms. The driver threw his hands up in frustration. He had a deadline to meet. None of the children not even her siblings, made a move to get her out of the road.

They all pumped their arms the more while chanting, "Blow your horn! Blow your horn!" The trucker finally heeded their signal since he didn't know if the little girl was playing an I double-dare you game. He pulled the cord to release the blast of the air horn. The noise was so loud that Aqueea's insides rattled. When she turned around, all she could see was the reflection of herself in the mirror-like bumper of the truck. She panicked. Dropping her book, she ran from one side of the bumper to the other. She couldn't seem to get away from it. She was paralyzed with fear. Tears streamed down her face; she couldn't get away from the truck. It was as if it surrounded her. The children and the trucker collapsed in laughter.

The driver yelled out of the window, "Will one of you please get her out of the road so I can get by!" Embarrassed, her older brother came to her rescue. He picked up her book, grabbed her by the hand, and yanked her out of the middle of the road.

"Serves you right," he admonished her. "That'll teach you about always having a book stuck up in your face."

Aqueea could now chuckle about that frightening childhood incident… and somehow, she still kept her fascination for eighteen-wheelers.

Her attention returned to what was going on outside her classroom window. She saw a worker climb up into the bulldozer's seat, and without hesitation, fired it up after it was off-loaded from the eighteen-wheeler. Its clawing treads left a clear rut in the earth behind it as it lumbered over to the tree stump.

Approaching the stump, the worker lowered the blade as he throttled up the engine of the bulldozer. Once the blade engaged the stump, it met with resistance. The stump refused to give up its place in the earth. Yet, like a dentist trying to break loose a tooth from its gum bed, the bulldozer's blade kept pushing and prodding the stump until the earth began to release its roots. Like a tooth being extracted, the stump finally broke loose. Looking at the stump lying on its side, its roots like bony, gnarled fingers of a witch who was reaching out to capture her tormentor, sadness swept over Aqueea.

Aqueea's eye caught the clock. In two minutes students were going to be coming in so she went to the classroom door, pushed it open, and stood outside, waiting to greet her students.

Later that day after school dismissed, she thought about the tree, the split logs, the branches, twigs, leaves, and the stump, but most of all, the gaping hole that resembled an open mouth crying for its lost occupant. The magnificent oak tree that had stood for decades, being nourished by Mother Earth, was gone. The scene of the unearthed tree haunted Aqueea. What did this ghost mean? Why couldn't she let go of what she'd seen... the power of the bulldozer, the resistance of the roots as it grabbed the earth and the earth, holding onto its occupant?

Come on girl, get a hold of yourself, she rebuked her thoughts. It was just a tree that was cut down and a stump that was uprooted for crying out loud!

Or was it? Deep down inside she pondered the question, *Were the stump's witch-like, decrepit root fingers grabbing at my mind because of some deeper meaning buried inside of me?*

Aqueea was amazed at how little time it took to annihilate something that had taken so long to grow. Frances Day's book, *America's Withering Branches*[50] came to her mind. Licentiousness, corruption, scandal, crime, amoral and asocial behavior, and inequities throughout society shook America to its very core in the waning years of the twentieth century. As our government appeared either unwilling or unable to deal with such problems, an increasingly disturbed populace cried out for solutions. "Slow down, America; evaluate progress, enjoy the beauty of its benefits, and allow everyone to get on board..." Day wrote.

Aqueea considered the millions of blacks who would have been uprooted yet another time if Abraham Lincoln had been successful in his lobby for compensated emancipation and deportation of the newly freed blacks. In breaking it down to enhancing the wages of white labor, he wrote...

---

[50] Day, Frances, America's Withering Branches, Vantage Press, New York, NY, 1995

"With deportation, even to a limited extent, enhanced wages to white labor is mathematically certain. Labor is like any other commodity in the market – increase the demand for it, and you increase the price of it. Reduce the supply of black labor, by colonizing the black laborer out of the country, and by precisely so much, you increase the demand for, and wages of, white labor."[51]

As Horton and Horton[52] wrote:

> "Emancipation was a matter of overt celebration in some places, and a slow culmination in others. But what freedom meant in 1863, how livelihood would change, how the masters would react, how freed people would find protection in the chaotic South, how they would meet potential rent payments, how agricultural laborers attached to the soil might now become owners of the land, and whether they would achieve citizenship rights were all unanswered questions during the season of emancipation. Joy mixed with uncertainty, songs of deliverance with expressions of fear."

President Lincoln's proposed permanent constitutional law for colonizing freed blacks did not pass, but other means have been developed to colonize blacks and limit their ability to have parity with the white community. For example, when Aqueea did some research on 2017's Most & Least Culturally

---

[51] Compensated Emancipation, http://www.mrlincolnfreedom.org

[52] Horton, James Oliver and Lois E. Horton, A History of the African American People, Smithmark Publishers, New York, NY, 1995

Diverse Cities,[53] she found that 501 of the largest cities were compared based on ethnicity and race, and then language and birthplace. Jersey City, New Jersey ranked number one. Next she wanted to see the percent of people who were born in some of the former slave states. The percent according to wallet hub were as follows: Alabama, 70.05; George, 54.89; Mississippi, 71.53; North Carolina, 57.14; South Carolina, 57.70; Virginia, 49.54. Next, she figured she'd take a look at the major American Cities with populations greater than four hundred thousand ranked by diversity white, black, Hispanic/Latino, Asian, other. According to information presented by *Priceonomic*,[54] Oakland, California had almost equal numbers of whites, blacks and Hispanic/Latinos. The same was true for Chicago, Illinois. Cities with a preponderance of whites were Sacramento, California; New York, New York; Boston, Massachusetts; San Diego, California; San Francisco, California; Fort Worth, Texas; Las Vegas, Nevada; Charlotte, North Carolina; Austin, Texas; Oklahoma, Oklahoma; Raleigh, North Carolina; Denver, Colorado; Jacksonville, Florida; Kansas, Missouri; Nashville-Davidson, Tennessee; Indianapolis, Indiana; Columbus, Ohio; Virginia Beach, Virginia; Settle, Washington; Mesa, Arizona; Omaha, Nebraska; Louisville/Jefferson County, Kentucky; Colorado Springs, Colorado and Portland, Oregon.

Cities that had a majority of blacks were Washington, D.C.; Atlanta, Georgia; Baltimore, Maryland; Memphis, Tennessee and Detroit, Michigan. Among the cities with the largest Hispanic/Latino populations were Long Beach, California;

[53] 2017's Most & Least Culturally Diverse Cities, https://wallethub.com
[54] The Most and Least Diverse Cities in America, https://priceonomics.com

Houston, Texas; Dallas, Texas; Fresno, California; Los Angeles, California; Albuquerque, New Mexico; San Antonio, Texas; Miami, Florida and El Paso, Texas. What *Priceonomic* called more balanced cities were Oakland, California; Chicago, Illinois and San Jose, California.

A 2000 American ethnicity map showing melting pots of ethnicities shows that African American or black is the second largest grouping with just over forty million people.[55] This article further stated, "For decades, the United States opened its doors and welcomed with open arms millions of immigrants who all arrived through New York's Ellis Island in the hope of a better life in America." In contrast to open arms, the article continues, "The majority of African Americans are descended from slaves from West and Central Africa and of course have become an integral part of the story of the United States, gaining the right to vote with the 15th amendment in 1870, but struggling with their civil rights for at least another century."

Finally, Aqueea decided to look at the Membership of the 113th Congress. Jennifer E. Manning, Information Research Specialist, reported that of African American members, there were forty-five (8.3 percent of the total membership) in the 113th Congress.[56] As she poured over the data, Aqueea could rationalize elements of Backcountry-English-Bourgeois and backcountry-frontier behavior filtering through. She perceived that according to the demographics, classism as it was in colonial times in terms of the ruling class having a hand in every aspect of society—the economy, and educational systems—still dominated as well as did

---

[55] American ethnicity map... http://www.dailymail.co.uk/news/article

[56] Membership of the 113th Congress: A Profile, Congressional Research Service, 7¬ 5700, www.crs.gov, R42964

poorer whites' hostility towards blacks. She could see what development planners had done in terms of promulgating colonies within current day America.

Robert Blauner, University of California, Berkeley in his paper Internal Colonialism and Ghetto Revolt[57] wrote:

> "There appear to be four basic components of the colonization complex. The first refers to how the racial group enters into the dominant society (whether colonial power or not). Colonization begins with a forced, involuntary entry. Second, there is an impact on the culture and social organization of the colonized people which is more than just a result of such natural processes as contact and acculturation. The colonizing power carries out a policy, which constrains, transforms, or destroys indigenous values, orientations, and ways of life. Third, colonization involves a relationship by which members of the colonized group tend to be administered by representatives of the dominant power…
>
> …A final fundament of colonization is racism. Racism is a principle of social domination by which a group seen as inferior or different in terms of alleged biological characteristics is exploited, controlled, and oppressed socially and psychically by a superordinate group."

---

[57] Blauner, Robert, a revised version of a paper delivered at the University of California Centennial Program, "Studies in Violence," Los Angeles, June 1, 1968

The foregoing demonstrates the behavior of the Backcountry-English-Bourgeois mentality of the ruling class and the Backcountry-frontier mentality of the poor whites.

Gregory D. Squires and Charis wrote an article entitled *Privileged Places*.[58] "Real estate mantra tells us that three factors determine the market value of a home: location, location, and location. The same could be said about the factors that determine the good life and people's access to it in metropolitan America. Place matters. Neighborhood counts. Access to decent housing, safe neighborhoods, good schools, useful contacts and other benefits is largely influenced by the community in which one is born, raised, and resides. Individual initiative, intelligence, experience, and all the elements of human capital are obviously important. Yet, understanding the opportunity structure in the United States today requires complementing where appropriate; altering the opportunity structure of the nation's urban communities is the role of race. Racial composition of neighborhoods has long been at the center of public policy and private practice in the creation and destruction of communities and in determining access to the elements of the good life, however defined. Place and race continue to be defining characteristics of the opportunity structure of metropolitan areas. Disentangling the impact of these two forces is difficult, if not impossible. However, where one lives and one's racial background are both social constructs that significantly shape the privileges (or lack thereof) that people enjoy."

Aqueea thought about what she'd read and what the people who wrote about and studied demographics encouraged her. For

---

[58] Race, Opportunity and Uneven Development in Urban America, Shelterforce Online, Issue #147, Fall 2006, http://nhi.org

example, 21ˢᵗ Century Demographics,[59] indicates that the U.S. Census Bureau predicts that by 2023 minority children will make the majority of schoolchildren, the majority of working-age Americans will be minorities by 2039, and minorities by 2042 will be a majority. With this in mind, Generation X-ers can turn the tide on what has been a long-standing practice in America by the Backcountry-English-Bourgeois mentality. This class has maintained its status quo place in the American society since the colonial period. They've held onto the decision-making processes regarding education, politics, economy, and demographics. The colonization plan that Thomas Jefferson and his peers set about to get freed blacks out of America didn't materialize and the deportation of freed blacks in President Lincoln's compensated emancipation plan didn't either. As a result, other means of colonizing the black population within the United States has been instituted. When one looks at demographics, the pattern seems to be large concentrations of blacks in the inner cities of America. It is not for some reason, but by a design that services, health, housing, education, playgrounds, etc., are not comparable to suburban communities. Jobs are available in the inner cities but not for inner cities' dwellers. They are available for the bedroom suburban communities that commute in and out of the inner cities.

A New People Generation

William G. Huitt, in his paper *"Success in the Conceptual Age: Another Paradigm Shift"*[60] wrote: "One of the primary functions of schooling is to prepare children and youth for adult success.

---

[59] 21st Century Demographics (21st century skills), http://www.centerforpubliceducation.org

[60] 32nd Annual Meeting of the Georgia Educational Research Association, Savannah, Ga., October 26, 2007, http://www.edpsyinteractive.org

However, as social and cultural changes occur, especially on a global level, so do the requirements for accomplishments... In each age, those individuals or social institutions that acquired the characteristics and resources necessary to take advantage of the new sources of wealth were able to enjoy a new standard of material living and social interaction. And now, just decades into the information age, it seems another profound change is occurring."

Aqueea thought about how savvy the teens in her alternative high school classes were with manipulating computers. They knew how to bypass firewalls, get to restricted sites, lock computers with their own passwords, find whatever information they were interested in, and download and save resources from the internet, including their favorite music. This generation, born between 1977 and 1994, and known as Generation Y[61] are incredibly sophisticated, technology wise, and immune to most traditional marketing and sales pitches. "... Gen Y are much more racially and ethnically diverse..."

Christian Bodewig indicates that basic cognitive skills should be a priority. It is pointed out that educational disadvantaged children are disproportionately exposed to quality education. "... interventions, can be an effective tool to make up for disadvantage by boosting students confidence and goal orientation." The article continues by indicating that "...With students captive in kindergarten and school during the critical period of their skills formation, innovation in classroom and teaching practices... can help foster advanced skills like problem-solving, critical thinking and team work."[62]

---

[61] Generations X, Y, Z and the Others, http://socialmarketing.org

[62] Bodewig, Christian, Preparing for the robots: Which skills for 21st century jobs? Tuesday, March 1, 2016, https://www.brookings.edu

Bodewig continues, "A worker's skill set has three components: cognitive skills like basic numeracy and literacy (including digital literacy), as well as advanced problem-solving and creative and critical thinking skills; social and behavioral skills like conscientiousness, grit, and openness to experience; and job- or occupation-specific technical skills like those required to work as an engineer or electrician... adults with poor literacy and numeracy skills have difficulty learning and updating the technical skills needed to compete in the modern job market."

Having taught nursery school as a YWCA volunteer, interacted with Title I teachers, kindergarten through fifth grade, worked with parents of Title I children, taught Adult High School/GED/Adult Basic Skills/ESL and Alternative High School, as well as several funded special programs such as a Mothers Are Special program (a literacy program for functionally illiterate mothers), Aqueea was familiar with the characteristics, skills, knowledge, and attitudes people in the black community lacked. She recognized that in order to become a New People, there were some hurdles that needed to be avoided such as classicism among blacks and some practices from the colonial period that would prove to be worthwhile such as teaching politics, economics, literacy, and a skill to every child.

She felt that one of the hurdles that need to be dealt with was a bourgeois class emerging among blacks. On an occasion when she and other business partners had sponsored a Private Business Reception (PBR) for new business partners, a new partner had brought someone with her to the reception, who was clearly a live-in domestic type person.

Upon seeing this person, Aqueea's up-line pulled her to the side and whispered in her ear, "Watch the caliber of people you bring in." Needless to say, Aqueea was taken aback by the remark. Aqueea, herself, had been raised in a community where people were quick to polarize each other. She thought about how in high school the guidance counselor gave kids who lived in town the best courses. For example, Aqueea had always dreamed of becoming a medical doctor, but because her parents were farmers, she never got the basic science and math classes that were needed in order to pursue medicine. She was put into an office proficiency track where she learned to type. When she looked back over her career as an educator, she had no regrets. She appreciated what John Steinbeck had to say about teachers: "I have come to believe that a great teacher is a great artist and that there are as few as there are any other great artists. Teaching might even be the greatest of the arts since the medium is the human mind and spirit."[63]

"I am a doctor after all," she often said to herself whenever she reflected on that high school dream. "I am a doctor; I evaluate; I prescribe a learning plan; I implement remediation therapy; I dispense medicines of skill acquisition to student patients, under my academic tutelage." A deep sense of satisfaction would always spread through her when she was reminiscent of that experience.

Another problem in the black community is that after getting on their feet, so to speak, large numbers of blacks leave the inner cities where they grew up and move to suburbia. There's nothing wrong with wanting to have a better place in which to live, but when some blacks move out, they turn their backs on what's left. Instead of using their advancement to advocate services for inner city children, many of them were busy themselves with the good life—cruises, club memberships, designer wardrobes and such.

---

[63] Steinbeck, John, Chicken Soup for the Soul Word-Finds, Volume 161, Inspiration 17

When asked about what adults could do for them, Aqueea's students said, "We think the grown-ups should spearhead cleanups, fix-ups, paint and restore public buildings, put in community gardens, make elected officials promote pride projects, create safe playgrounds and organize fun activities after school and in the summer for all kids." They told her, "We want some place where we can be kids. Kids are supposed to be safe, play, and have fun." These student classroom discussions moved Aqueea, especially since they were fifteen, sixteen, and seventeen years old, some of whom were already parents and most of the males, on ankle-bracelets. What she perceived she was hearing was that these young people had never had the chance to be children. Aqueea thought, *What if every high school graduate, every college graduate, every professional who was from the hood, everybody who had escaped the black ghettoes of America came back and beautified the life of someone left behind? What if roach, rat, and mice infested, absentee landlord buildings were buildings with garden terraces, colorful curb-appeal and not jail-like cement block tenements stacked like towers in the sky? And what if elected officials passed laws to require space for recreation and learning centers in housing complexes? What if urban planners and demographers worked with community leaders to plan a landscape of beautiful functional cities—cities throughout the country—but no camouflaged colonization ghettoes?* Aqueea reasoned, *What if like Harlem, during its renaissance which was transformed into a black city within the city of New York with black intellectuals, theaters, clubs and restaurants, schools and effective political leaders, churches and respected spiritual leaders, medical doctors, dentists, mom and pop stores, markets, banks, jobs, etc.—all of the economies necessary for a self-sufficient community—black ghettoes were transformed and emerged as a community of New People?*

A New Clan

America has created a new clan of blacks born out of the ones slave masters bred. They are devoid of their African roots. Like the roots of the oak tree stump's root fingers, they reached up with gnarled, twisted appendages seeking nourishment and comfort. These hybrids have been fed the American culture, but their appendages after partaking of this new culture have found that they are like shadows in the mid-day sun. Though the ruling class's mores have been absorbed by them in daily life, in textbooks, the media, holidays, and every other aspect of sociological and physiological fibre of being Americanized, neither their presence nor their value have been validated. As a result, blacks are no more than shadows in the management of America. The idea of a Birthright American was birthed in Aqueea's mind. She was released from her childhood questioning. She was freed that day in an ESL workshop that focused on Preventive Mental Health in the ESL Classroom. As she watched her fellow white Americans thumbtacking their European roots, she discovered within herself the answer to her youthful question, "Who Am I?" She was a Birthright, American-African. By her birth, she was American. By her socialization she was American, but by the color of her skin she was African. She was a Birthright-Virginian-American-African.

The African part of her began unfolding when she and her older son joined a church that was ninety-five percent African. She'd noticed that her next-door neighbors, who were African, always dressed in elegant African attire on Sundays.

One day she inquired of her neighbor, Grace, "Why do you dress so elegantly?" "It is our culture," Grace replied. Grace, a nurse, and her husband, a pharmacist, would travel forty miles north from the country-burb community they and Aqueea lived in. As they continued to talk once they'd met, Aqueea learned that the church they attended was in the same urban area where she taught. For fifteen years, Aqueea traveled forty miles, one-way, daily from her country-burb townhouse to go to work. After her husband's death, she moved back to the city. That was when she decided to check out Grace's church; she found that it was only two blocks from her son's house. The first time Aqueea and her son walked into the Presbyterian Church, she felt a deep-seated stirring in her spirit. The congregation was singing in some language she didn't know but the tune of what was being sung was that of a well-known hymn so she and her son started singing the hymn in English. After a few visits and talking with the pastor, an African, she and her son joined. Their intent was to offer some of their American culture to the congregants who were 95 percent immigrants. Only five of the more than two hundred members were not from Africa. At least a dozen different African languages were spoken among the people and there were several African tribes and clans among the membership. Later, the congregation elected Aqueea as an elder and her son, as a deacon. They participated in many African traditional celebrations, which included outdooring ceremonies for newborn babies. Aqueea learned that a part of a baby's name was for the day of the week the child was born. Since she and her older son were born on a Wednesday and her younger son was born on a Friday, their names were Akua (which happened to sound like Aqueea), Kwaku, and Kofi, respectively. These names were in the Twi language, one of the African languages spoken in the congregation.

Aqueea learned many things about the deep culture of the African people in the congregation through firsthand experiences with them. For example, she found that there really were tribal kings, queens, and chiefs. At several events she and her son had attended such as funerals, weddings, retirements, and birthdays, they saw tribal leaders, gold chains draped over their shoulders reaching down to the floor and gold rings on their fingers and toes being escorted to their choice banquet seats by tribal chiefs and elders. They were followed by queen mothers and their court, all of them wearing breath-taking jewelry and elegant garments of lace, Kenta cloth, linen, and brocades.

She also came across what she called a new segregation. When her son had been laid off, he went to the pastor to ask for referrals to job openings since he knew that many congregants had gotten jobs through him. Basically the pastor told him that he could do nothing for him and that being an American, he should have no trouble finding a job. She and her son began to see the African network—their communal meetings, their business customers, their communities within communities, (doctors, lawyers, dentists, accountants, auto repair shops, nurses, educators)—was the Africans' venue for reaching back to help each other, especially their tribal people. The colonial fiat, the ruling class had for training orphans and bastards in a trade so that they could support themselves and how the status quo had formed a network of control for them and those like them came to her mind.

She deeply understood her skin color while with the African community too. On many occasions when she was wearing African apparel, she was mistaken as being African, especially Ghanaian. When she had her Ancestry DNA[64] done, it showed that her ethnicity estimate was twenty-nine percent Ivory Coast/Ghana;

---

[64] Ancestry DNA Ethnicity, http://dna.ancestry.com

twenty-eight percent Cameroon/Congo; nine percent Nigeria; five percent Benin/Togo; three percent Mali; three percent Senegal; two percent Africa South-Central Hunter-Gatherers; two percent Africa North and one percent Africa Southeastern Bantu. Knowing the complexity of tribes, languages, and customs of the African peoples, Aqueea was even more convinced that she and others like her who were descendants from the new breed of blacks that slave owners bred were a New Clan, American-Africans.

As American-Africans, Aqueca reasoned, *we must undertake the task of defining who we are ourselves. We must reach back and uplift the least among us too—the orphans, the bastards—and teach them a trade and literacy. But how do we do that?* She came across an article, *"13 Essential 21st Century Skills for Today's Students"*[65] that advised parents that children need to improve twenty-first century skills in order to be successful participants in the global economy, college, and work. Development in four critical areas were cited: Collaboration and teamwork; Creativity and imagination; Critical thinking; and problem solving. Other critical skills for success were: Flexibility and adaptability; Global and cultural awareness; Information literacy; and Leadership. It reported that: Civic literacy and citizenship; Oral and written communication skills; Social responsibility and ethics; Technology literacy and Initiative are second tiers of important 21st Century Skills.

The Center for Public Education, September 21, 2009[66], indicated:

The organization man is long gone. For one thing, the organization that created him has disappeared. In large corporations especially, the traditional top-down hierarchy has shifted to a flat-

---

[65] https://www.envision.com, January 9, 2014

[66] The 21st Century job (21st century skills), http://www.centerforpubliceducation.org

ter organizational structure. Less supervision, more autonomy, more collaboration, and less predictability mean that today's students will need to be independent problem-solvers in order to succeed at their jobs. In a global knowledge economy, these companies realize, human capital is their most important resource. As a result, jobs — especially those in globally competitive firms are changing in four ways:

- Less hierarchy and supervision
- More Autonomy and responsibility
- More collaboration
- Less predictability and stability

As the CEO of UPS described it in 2005, "We look for [employees] who can learn how to learn."

NEW CLAN EDUCATION: AMERICAN-AFRICANS

"And one of the elders answered saying unto me, What are these which are arrayed in white robes? and whence came they?

And I said unto him, Sir, thou knowest. And he said to me, These are they which came out of great tribulation, and have washed their robes, and made them white in the blood of the Lamb."

Revelation 7: 13–14
Authorized King James Version

Aqueea, in answering the question, "Who am I?" and choosing to label herself as a Virginian American-African, considered the argument she probably would get from black intellects. For example, Lawrence C. Ross, Jr. wrote: "...it is exceeding important for all Africans within the Diaspora to constantly reassert their African roots... it is a cultural inheritance that was paid for in blood... To forget or disassociate is to allow those who stole us to ultimately succeed in separating our people from humanity..."[67]

Aqueea felt that before she could delve into the African Experience, she wanted to focus on American-African blacks, descendants of captured slaves, Birthright Americans. Immigrants from countries of the Diaspora, after becoming naturalized citizens of the United States, call themselves after their countries: Jamaican-American, Haitian-American, Nigeria-American or Ghanaian-American. Birthright American-Africans can say, as stated in the National Negro Hymn: "...We have come over a way that with tears has been watered, We have come, treading our path thro' the blood of the slaughtered..."[68]

Immigrant blacks bring with them to America, their language, culture, social customs, etc., and tend to group themselves together. To Birthright American-Africans another form of segregation—a new segregation was discernable to Aqueea. She recalled the time when Kwaku, an accountant, was working for a major oil company at one of its refineries. As a matter of practices, employees had to participate in safety drills. Kwaku noticed the young black man, an engineer who participated in the drills, always avoided Kwaku. One day the two had to work together dur-

---

[67] Ross, Jr., Lawrence, The Ways of Black Folks, page xii, Kensington Publishing Corp., New York, NY, 2003

[68] Johnson, James Weldon, R. Rosemond Johnson, Lift Every Voice and Sing

ing a drill, which necessitated the need for them to speak. As a result they continued to communicate. Learning that Michael and his wife lived only minutes from his mom and himself before he bought his own home, Kwaku invited Michael and his wife, Christine, to dinner. During dinner, Michael told Kwaku and Aqueea that he had been told by whites to stay away from American blacks because they were ignorant, lazy, and uneducated. He was surprised to find that both Kwaku and Aqueea had advanced degrees, lived in a well articulated townhouse in an upscale community, and displayed the social skills that he saw in the circle of contacts his wife, the daughter of a diplomat, had grown up in.

Another example of this new segregation was towards Kofi. He told of a bakery he would always stop by before going to work. The owner, an African immigrant, never spoke to him to even say good morning or looked him in the face. One day, he had forgotten to take his name badge off the lapel of his jacket. He noticed that the woman was staring at his lapel with a look of amazement on her face. Thinking that he had something on his jacket, when he looked down, he saw that she'd been reading his ID badge, which had his name, followed by Ph.D., Professor, School of Business and the name of the university. In spite of this discovery, the woman still didn't show Kofi any hospitality. Kofi and his wife, a Cape Verde immigrant, always hosted a Christmas dinner for young families in their neighborhood because they had no family members nearby. One of the couples was from West Africa. Following a Christmas dinner, after everyone had left except this couple, Aqueea asked if it were true that white Americans told them to avoid socializing with American blacks. Sadly, they said, "Yes."

In her interaction with black immigrants, Aqueea found that many of them knew nothing about American history or of the struggles of Birthright Americans, those bred by slave owners and their descendants. For instances, President Abraham Lincoln in 1863 ordered twenty thousand acres of land to be sold to freed-man in twenty-acre plots. This came in part as a result of an unsuccessful deportation plan that had been on record since Thomas Jefferson's era. Salmon Chase, Secretary of the Treasury, increased the acreage that President Lincoln had ordered to forty acres per family. The twenty black leaders who met with General William T. Sherman in 1865 told him that land ownership would provide security for the newly freed slaves. Sherman's Special Field Order No.15 reserved four hundred thousand acres on the coastal land of South Carolina and Georgia for black settlement. Sherman also loaned the settlers military mules. Yet following the assassination of President Lincoln and becoming President, Andrew Johnson returned the land to the former owners.[69]

Like the opportunity lost during the indentured servants era and the Revolutionary War period, again, the establishment of black self-sufficiency, political representation, economics, education, and a voice in the American society was denied. From the beginning, America has never wanted blacks to have equal footing with whites. From Thomas Jefferson's contrived philosophy of racial prejudice, the ruling class has continued to subjugate blacks to roadblocks, which obstruct the acquisition of the American Dream. Among these roadblocks are inner city ghettoes with inadequate educational systems, decaying roach, mice and rat infested housing that have absentee landlords; drugs and guns (that

---

[69] Forty Acres and a Mule – The Black Past: Remembered and Reclaimed, http://www.black-past.org

blacks don't have the means for bringing into the country), and finally, Pipelines-to-Prison and Schools-to-Prison. Pipelines-to-Prison and Schools-to-Prison are set up to snare young black males and funnel them into the penal system, thereby robbing them of the chance for becoming productive citizens and the ability to vote. As a result, they are having little or no meaningful representation from elected officials or the capacity to acquire the American Dream. In addition, the penal pipeline becomes a boomerang, designed to return the ex-con back to prison.

The Birthright American-Africans, especially those of Generation Y, born between 1977 and 1994, have the full opportunity to pursue the American Dream: an education, a job, a home, and a family or however they want to define their American Dream, because of the diversity that is accepted among them. They have the chance to take hold of the privilege of being American-Africans and possessing what is entitled to every American: life, liberty and the pursuit of happiness.

Aqueea pondered what could be done to help Virginian American-Africans, North Carolinians, South Carolinians, and Georgians—any Birthright American-African whose African roots have been bred out of them.

I think, Aqueea said to herself, *that the focus on discovering African ancestry DNA might be another way the ruling class network could be trying to distract the minds of Birthright American-Africans from seeking parity in America—our country. From the beginning it has always been about economics and land ownership.* Aqueea recalled the quest for land acquisition in colonial America and she, now, fully appreciated her parents for their acquisition of the farm—the place and Mr. Larks for selling it to her dad.

She pulled out a writing pad. "What can I can say to my fellow descendants of survivors of the Middle Passage?" she asked herself. She remembered something she'd read entitled: *A Mega-Experiment in Jewish Education: The Impact of Birthright israel*, conceived with the hope that engagement with Israel would strengthen participants Jewish identities and counter the threat to Jewish continuity.[70] The purpose of this mega-experiment was to re-connect Jewish youths with their heritage. Aqueea wondered what young blacks would do if they really knew America, from sea to shining sea.

THE WRITING PAD

"Tell ye your children of it, and let your children tell their children, and their children another generation..."

Joel 1:3
Authorized King James Version

"Thank you researchers of the Birthright israel project, for your report," she wrote. "I'd never thought of the birthright that fellow descendants of the slave trade and I have in America. I was much taken aback when I found about the colonization attempts and I'm glad they failed." She thought about the scripture in the Old Testament in the Book of Joel. Not only that, she considered how the Jewish people had been commanded by God to teach from generation to

---

[70] Saxe, L., Kadushin, C., Kelner, S., Rosen, M., and Yereslove, E. (2001). A Mega-Experiment in Jewish Education: The Impact of Birthright israel. (Birthright israel Summary Report 1). Waltham, MA: Brandeis University, Cohen Center for Modern Jewish Studies.

generation how they'd been delivered from their enemies and oppressors. In talking with her high school students, she'd found that most of them could not tell of their parents or grandparents past because when they asked, they were told to forget about it.

"There's nothing to talk about. Who wants to talk about outhouses for toilets, or getting water from a spring to cook, wash and bathe with? Who wants to talk about going to the back doors of restaurants?" Surprisingly, none of the students had someone they knew who had participated in The March on Washington, something that Aqueea and her husband did and twenty years later, took their sons with them to the second march.

When Aqueea had spoken with a co-worker about the Civil Rights Movement, the person said to her, "Get over it!" an admonishment that Snadhya Rani Jha mentioned in her book *Pre-Post-Racial America.*[71]

"What would I write as a curriculum for Birthright American-Africans?" she mused. "I definitely would include visitations to black historic places such as the National Museum of African American History & Culture in Washington, DC and the Harlem section of New York." She chuckled at the time the class was speculating about the reinstatement of the Draft. One student said he'd leave the country.

When asked where he'd go, his reply was, "I'd run away to California." Of course, his classmates ribbed him, but Aqueea understood. Many of the students had little knowledge of the vastness of America; some had never been outside the school neighborhood they lived in. She paired the student up with a classmate volunteer who took him to the world map Aqueea had

---

[71] Jha, Sandhya Rani, Pre-Post-Racial America, Chalice Press, St. Louis, Missouri, 2015

mounted on one wall of her classroom. The classmate showed him where he was on the east coast and where California was, on the west coast. Like most of her students, Aqueea was not surprised that the young man was deficient in his knowledge of American geography and American history as well. He could, on the other hand, handle himself quite proficiently on the streets. He had already, because of his truancy, disruptive behavior in school, infractions with the law, and gang affiliation, began his journey towards the pipeline of school-to-prison.

Aqueea felt that a Birthright American-African course of study could provide the re-orientation he needed as well as most inner-city students, to get off the downward spiral to disenfranchisement. Terry L. Richardson and Timothy Levi Jones on juvenile justice wrote: "End the school-to-prison pipeline for children of color... The disparities in our youth prisons reflect the same systemic racism that infects our adult incarceration system."[72]

She would include civics, demographics, employability skills, and the feats of blacks like Bunker Hill, The Tuskegee Airmen, etc.—black presence in all the wars of America. Also, included would be slave narratives, congressional records as well as journal notes and letters the ruling classes wrote pertaining to slavery. "I would teach them how to use the U.S. Census Bureau records to start a name search for their family," she wrote, "and help them create their own motto and philosophy of life."

A COAT OF ARMS

Like Dr. Henry Louis Gates, Jr. wrote in *Finding Oprah's Roots*, page twenty-two, Aqueea also looked at ads of coat of arms that

---

[72] The Star-Ledger, Affiliated with NJ.com, Friday, March 10, 2017, page 14

were advertised in magazines when she was a teen and wondered what one would be like for her family name. What she had learned was that *"any pictorial badge which is used by an individual or a family with the meaning that it is a badge indicative of that person or family and adopted and repeatedly used in that sense, is heraldic.*[73] "What better way to trace and record my genealogy?" she said to herself.

Aqueea knew that she was a Virginian Birthright American-African because in 1850, her family name was that of multiple slave-owning family members. She had no doubt that they were growing their own slaves because of the backcountry-ness of Mecklenburg County, especially at the extreme southwestern part of the county where she was born and reared. Furthermore, she deduced that she was about five generations removed from slavery. She figured that based on Grandpa Hamily's date of birth, his grandfather would have been born before the Emancipation Proclamation. Thinking about the coat of arms she'd seen in magazines as a teen, she decided that she would create her own.

A lot of thought was put into what her coat of arms would look like. She rationalized that since she and her older son were under the zodiac sign of Leo, and her husband and younger son, the sign of Capricorn, these could represent the family's supporters. The Capricorn had only one foot mounted on the shield of the coat of arms to signify that her husband had passed away. She used the slave ship as a reminder that her ancestor had survived the Middle Passage, five white waves to represent the five generations she was removed from slavery, and two black waves to represent the sharks that trailed the slave ships. The MCMXLI and

---

[73] Fox-Davies, A. C., A Complete Guide to Heraldry, Skyhorse Publishing, Inc., 2007

the HLDG in the helm, were to represent her date of birth and her name. She chose the globe to represent the phrase she and her Russian teacher had created, Living in the World as At Home and At Home as in the World, to represent her view of oneness. The Cross was to symbolize that Jesus Christ's death and resurrection made it possible for all men to be free in Him and the Bible in the crest.

She chose as her motto scroll, the Latin term *Per Angusta Ad Augusta* which means "through difficulties to honor" to reflect the ancestral journey of her people and as a perspective for her posterity, a fleurs-de-lis for mantling and green grass for the compartment.

She used the Old Testament Nehemiah 7:5 to answer why she wanted to create an artifact for her posterity:

> "And my God put into mine heart to gather together the nobles, and the rulers, and the people, that they might be reckoned by genealogy..."

> Nehemiah 7:5
> Authorized King James Version

Aqueea, having written the last of her innermost thoughts, put her writing utensil down and closed the writing pad. She pushed her chair back, got up from the table, and walked toward the front door of her little country house. She stepped out onto the screened-in porch, pulled the protective cover from the wicker rocking chair, and fluffed the seat cushions. It was getting towards evening; the sun was quickly sinking behind the Leland pines.

Settling contently into the chair, she began humming a tune, watching for the deer that would soon come out of the woods to graze in the meadow beyond her yard before disappearing in the underbrush along Buffalo Creek.

As twilight closed in on the landscape and Venus shone like a blue-white diamond in the sky, Aqueea got up from the wicker rocker, covered it again, and went back inside to prepare her dinner. As she looked out the kitchen window at the night sky, as if the herald angels had joined her, she broke into singing the tune she had been humming:

> "My country 'tis of thee,[74]
> Sweet land of liberty,
> Of thee I sing:
> Land where my fathers died,
> Land of the pilgrims' pride,
> From ev'ry mountainside
> Let Freedom ring!"

---

[74] Smith, Samuel Francis; From Thesaurus Musicus, 1744, Source Unknown

References Cited

-2017's Most & Least Culturally Diverse Cities; https://wal-lethub.com

-21st Century Demographics (21st Century Skills), http://centerforpubliceducation.org

-32nd Annual Meeting of the Georgia Educational Research Association, Savannah, Ga., October 26, 2007, http://www.edpsycinteractive.org

-American Ethnicity Map…, http://www.dailymail.co.uk/news/article

-Ancestry DNA Ethnicity, http://dna.ancestry.com

-Banneker, Benjamin, Thomas Jefferson and the Question of Racism… https://www.everydaycitizen.com

-Blauner, Robert, a revised version of a paper delivered at the University of California Centennial Program, "Studies in Violence," Los Angeles; June 1, 1968

-Bodewig, Christian, Preparing for the robots: Which Skills for 21st Century jobs?, Tuesday, March 1, 2016, https://www.brookings.edu

-Compensated Emancipation, http://www.mrlincolnfreedom.org

-County Spine District, Page 983, Nov. 29, 1850 Census Record, Abrahams Planes Dist., Dec. 14, 1850

-Day, Frances, *America's Withering Branches*, Vantage Press, New York, NY, 1995

-Forty Acres and a Mule-The Black Past: Remembered and Reclaimed, http://www.blackpast.org

-Fox-Davies, A. C., *A Complete Guide to Heraldry*, Skyhorse Publishing, Inc., 2007

-Freepages.genelogy.rootsweb.ancestry.com/ajac/vamecklenburg, Transcriber, Tom Blake, August 2003

-Gates, Henry Louis, *Finding Oprah's Roots, Finding Your Own*, Crown Publishers, New York, 2007

-Generations X, Y, Z and the Others, http://socialmarketing.org

-Gentry in Colonial Virginia; http: www.enclopediavirginia.or

-George Washington's Mount Vernon, http://www.mountvernon.org

-Horton, James Oliver, and Lois E. Horton, *A History of the African American People*, Smithmark Publishers, New York, NY, 1995

-http://dickinsonproject.rch.uky.edu/bgraphy.php

-http://www.encyclopediavirginia.org/Carter_Robert_1728-1804

-https://www.envisionexperience.com, January 9, 2014

-https://www.history.com/topics/us-presidents/thomas-jefferson

-https://onkwehonwerising.files.wordpress.com/2013/04/settlers-mythology-of-the-white-proletariat.pdf

-https://www.nytimes.com/2005/08/07/books/review/setting-them-fr…

-Jha, Sandhya Rani, *Pre-Post-Racial America*, Chalice Press, St. Louis, Missouri, 2015

-Johnson, James Weldon, R. Rosemond Johnson, *Lift Every*

Voice and Sing

-Lockett, Dr. Arnold, *Stolen Identities, Where are the Lost African Tribes?* 2004

-Majors, Geraldyn, *Black Society*, Johnson Publishing Company, Inc., 1976

-Membership of the 113th Congress: A Profile, Congressional Research Service, 7-5700, www.crs.gov, R42946

-National Register of Historic Places, Clarksville Historic District, Page 65

-Prestwould Plantation, http://www.aahistoricsiteva.org

-*Race, Opportunity and Uneven Development in Urban America*, Shelterforce Online, Issue #147, Fall 2006, http://nhi.org

-Ross, Jr., Lawrence, *The Ways of Black Folks*, page xii, Kensington Publishing Corp., New York, NY 2003

-Saxe, L., Kadushin, C., Kelner, S., Rosen, M., & Yereslove, E. (2001). *A Mega-Experiment in Jewish Education: The Impact of Birthright israel*. (Birthright israel Summary Report 1). Waltham, MA: Brandeis University, Cohen Center for Modern Jewish Studies.

-Shadows on the Roanoke-William-Byrd-Buffalo Springs, https://www.discoversouthside.com

-Smith, Samuel Francis, From *Thesaurus Musicus*, 1744, Source Unknown

-Steinbeck, John, *Chicken Soup for the Soul Word-Finds*, Volume 161, Inspiration 17

-The 21st Century job (21st Century Skills), http://www.centerforpubliceducation.org

-The Most and Least Diverse Cities in America, https://priceonomics.com

-The Star-Ledger, Affiliated with NJ.com, Friday, March 10, 2017, page 14

-*The Underclass: Breaking The Cycle*, Time, October 10, 1988

-Traywick, Jr., H. H., *Empire of the Owls*, Dementi Milestone Publishing, Inc., Manakin-Sabot, VA, 2013

-Washington, Booker T. *Up from Slavery: An Autobiography*, Doubleday, Page & Co., NY, 1901

-Watkins Family Information from Andy Watkins_awinkins6@gmail.com

-Wiencek, Henry, *An Imperfect God: George Washington, His Slaves, and the Creation of America*, Farrar, Straus and Giroux, New York, 2004

-www.history.com/topics/american-civic-war/black-leaders-during-reconstruction

-www.oprah.com/oprahshow/emmitt_traces_his_family_history

Recommended Readings

Achebe, Chinua, *Things Fall Apart*, Marco Book Company, 2007

Edwards, Lillie, Ph.D., Drew University, Madison, New Jersey, E. Obiri Addo, Ph.D., Drew University, Madison, New Jersey, **Teacher's Guide**, *Things Fall Apart*, Chinua Achebe, **and Related Readings**, EVERBIND Anthologies, Lodi, New Jersey

Haley, Alex, *Queen*, Reader's Digest Condensed Books, Volume 1; Pleasantville, New York, 1994

Levy, Andrew, *The First Emancipator*, Random House, New York, NY, 2005

Miers, Earl Schenck, ***The Last Campaign,*** *Grant Saves the Union*, J. B. Lippincott, Co., Philadelphia & New York, 1972

Thomas, Hugh, *Slave Trade*, Simon & Schuster, New York, NY, 1997

Paris, Peter J., *The Spirituality of African People*, Fortress Press, Minneapolis, MN, 1995

Hill, Lawrence, *The Book of Negroes*, W.W. Norton & Co., New York, NY, 2007

Pinkett, Randal and Jeffery Robinson, *Black Faces in White Places: 10 Game-Changing Strategies to Achieve Success and Find Greatness*, Amacom American Management Association, New York, NY, 2011

Wilkerson, Isabel, *The Warmth of Other Suns*, Random House Publishing Group, Random House, Inc., 2010

The Farm House

The original two-room, two-floor structure (far end),
circa 1750's style

A corridor porch, added on later, connects the original
house to a dining room and kitchen.

Hallie L. Gamble

Top Photo: left to right, (Chicken Coop, Corncrib, Toolshed)

Bottom Photo: left to right, Cow Shed, Corncrib, Stable,
background; Pigpen, foreground